# SLIVERS OF LIFE

## A Collection of Short Stories

# SLIVERS OF LIFE

## A Collection of Short Stories

### Beem Weeks

# SLIVERS OF LIFE
## A Collection of Short Stories

Copyright © 2014, 2016

Fresh Ink Group
An Imprint of:
The Fresh Ink Group, LLC
PO Box 525
Roanoke, TX  76262
Email: info@FreshInkGroup.com
www.FreshInkGroup.com

Edition 1.0  2014
Edition 1.1  2016

Book design by Ann E. Stewart

Cover design by M.A. Manzoor & Stephen Geez / Fresh Ink Group



Cataloging-in-Publication Recommendations: General Fiction; Historical Fiction; Short Stories; Coming of Age; Alzheimer's Disease; Vampires; Teenagers; Troubled Teenagers; Young Adults; Cutters; Murder; Doughboys; World War One; Rock Star

Library of Congress Control Number: 2014950312

ISBN-13: 978-1-936442-20-1

To Lisa, Darin, and Mom

# Acknowledgements

Stephen Geez; Ann Stewart; Everybody at Fresh Ink Group; Y. Correa; Monica F. Brown-Martinez (Queen of Spades); Nonnie Jules and the entire Rave Reviews Book Club; Brendon Moorhouse, Ian Fenny, and the entire community at Koobug.com; Jane Yates; Sienna Rose; Everybody at Writing.com; And to the incredible poet Cloudsgrey (Kelly Jean Rice).

# Table of Contents

# A MATCH MET

Nobody around these parts could ever recall a time when Charlie Tricklett had been anything less than fit as a proverbial fiddle. Even as a child, when every other kid in the fifth grade over at Sumpterville Elementary School let those Gawd-awful chicken pox come home to roost, amazing Charlie didn't find a single bump on his skin. So it became quite a curious thing when the man took to his sickbed late last month.

Now, nobody expected much would come of this rare bout with illness. It started right after Charlie had gone to bed one evening after his nightly pipe. He smoked out on his front porch, the way he'd done for most of his adult life. Next morning, though, the man complained of a busy stomach. Like maybe he'd ate a thing or two that didn't quite sit well with him.

"I'll get over this in a few hours," Charlie told his wife Elmira. "It ain't like I'm dying."

Elmira just gave up a short nod, handed the man his pipe, thus granting her approval for a rare indoor smoke.

Two days later old Charlie hadn't gotten any better. In fact, some might even say the man had taken a turn for the worse. He'd gone past vomiting, pushing up only air and a little spit from time to time. He didn't bother with food or drink, either; it'd only just have come right back up.

Two weeks into his ordeal Charlie sought the advice of Doctor Ronanberg—a rare occurrence indeed! The only time the good doctor ever entered the Tricklett home was on those once-monthly Friday night poker games.

Doc Ronanberg gave the man a thorough twice-over, gathering statistical details on things referred to as vitals, swiping a fair amount of blood and urine—of which old Charlie was none-too-pleased to part—before proclaiming the situation perplexing.

"Suppose it's some new plague," Charlie suggested to his wife. "Maybe they'll name it after me if I die from it."

"Doubtful," is all Elmira said of the subject, handing the man his nightly pipe.

*     *     *

The good people of Sumpterville took turns helping put Charlie's crops into his fields. The man himself couldn't so much as raise his head up off his pillow by that third week. But there'd be food on the table come harvest.

"Never could stand the smell of that awful poison," Charlie said, concerning the stink of herbicide coming off the freshly turned field next to the house. "Always makes me sick to my stomach."

*     *     *

By the end of the month, Charlie had reached his end. All the life had sneaked away during the previous weeks, leaving the man ready for his face-to-face with the Almighty.

It was here, on what would most certainly be his deathbed, that Charlie opted to ease his conscience, to make confession of what he'd been up to during that last month before he took sick.

"Elmira," he proclaimed in his weak and pitiful voice. "I've been carrying on with Virginia Slocum up the road. It's only been just recently, but I'm most guilty of sin."

Elmira, with a grin upon her thin lips, leaned in close to her husband of twenty-five years and whispered sweetly into his ear. "I already knew that, Charlie. That's why I've been putting all that herbicide in your pipe tobacco."

*     *     *

Charlie had gone on to his maker by the time old Doctor Ronanberg discovered the high amounts of herbicide in those blood and urine samples. And since Charlie had been a life-long man of the fields, his death would go down as a hazard of the farming trade.

And what of Elmira?

Well, she sold off the farm, bought herself a plane ticket to Florida, and found her own face-to-face with the Almighty when that same airplane came down unexpectedly in a farmer's field just outside of Atlanta.

# Lost Boy

Joey Gossmer was just four years old when his dad brought that trampoline home one evening after work. Had it piled in the back of his truck, he did. Almost immediately the cry of springs filled the neighborhood with its *Shweek! Shweek! Shweek!*

Some people—like Mr. Spellman next door—didn't appreciate the noisy intrusion on the once-quiet tree-lined street. "How's a guy supposed to even think?" he'd often say to anybody foolish enough to lend ear to his frequent complaints. But Mr. Spellman, he complained about a lot of things—most notably the Wisickis' poodle, who often traipsed through the Spellman's backyard on its way home from early morning wanderings, leaving little piles in its wake.

That trampoline, though, *that's* what really riled the old man to no end.

"Let it go, Max," Mrs. Spellman would tell her husband. "He's just a little boy."

"He's a young hoodlum, you ask me. I mean, just *listen* to that infernal racket."

*Shweek! Shweek! Shweek!*

The din would not be ignored.

Mr. Spellman hollered at the youthful offender from his own side of the backyard fence, thought to put a little fear into the unruly lad, maybe intimidate him into avoiding that stupid contraption altogether.

That boy, though, young Joey, he'd taken after his mother, a stubborn girl who'd grown up in this very neighborhood.

"I ain't scared of you," he hollered right back at Mr. Spellman. "Mom says you're just a miserable old man."

Max bristled at the rebuttal. "Oh! I am, am I?" He'd show that silly little brat the very definition of miserable. "Keep up with that racket and we'll see what happens!"

*Shweek! Shweek! Shweek!*

*    *    *

Max Spellman called the police four times that first week, laid claim to the taxpayer's right to be free from harassment and thuggery. Nothing ever got done about it, though; the troublemaker remained free to upset the natural balance of the way things ought to be.

*Shweek! Shweek! Shweek!*

It was a simple idea, a bold stroke of genius that struck Max Spellman during one of his afternoon power naps.

"I'll show *him*," he said, rushing toward the shed in the backyard.

The garden hose reached to the fence; the sprinkler would certainly toss water on that worthless contraption—and it would soak that little blond-headed tyrant as well.

And it worked, too—for a day. The boy's father, he got wise to the plan that evening and moved the trampoline to the other corner of their yard, far away from the deepest reach of Max Spellman's garden hose.

But that sound—sound carries, dammit!

*Shweek! Shweek! Shweek!*

"It's not nearly as loud as it had been, Max," Mrs. Spellman told her husband.

Oh, but the man could still hear it. That's all it took to put him on the road to Crazyville.

"I'll go over there after dark and dump gasoline on the thing and set it afire!" Max promised.

His wife had other notions, though. "You'll do no such thing, Maxwell Jordan Spellman!"

That was that. Defeat filled the old-timer's head.

Beaten by a child.

*Shweek! Shweek! Shweek!*

*   *   *

Sirens yanked Max Spellman from his afternoon power nap. The urgent shriek tore into that brief moment of silence when the boy would be down for his own midday doze.

"Where's it at, Margie?" Max hollered from his room.

Margie Spellman, the girl he'd first fallen in love with nearly sixty years earlier, settled into the doorway, that look of loss splashed across her face. "It's an ambulance."

"I didn't ask *what* it is," Max answered, pulling himself from his bed, "I asked *where* it is."

"Up at the top of the street," she said, laying each word softly in its proper place.

The Milfords, Max thought. They'd been in the neighborhood nearly as long as the Spellmans. And that Nita Milford, she wasn't exactly the healthiest soul to be found. Of course, it didn't have to be Nita. It could very well be Stanton Milford; the old geezer had to be pushing eighty years by now.

But Margie shoved those notions to the side. She said, "The Milfords are on vacation in Florida this week."

*   *   *

Joey Gossmer was just four years old when he died. He'd been hit by a car whose driver assumed she could handle a quick text message while passing through the neighborhood. She ended up on the sidewalk, though, she, and that car of hers.

And Joey, the little boy from right next door, he'd just been riding his bicycle, giving that trampoline a rest, allowing Mr. Spellman a bit of afternoon peace.

*   *   *

Max Spellman sat up in his bed, unable to capture his usual midday power nap. Sleep of any sort had eluded him since that awful day two weeks earlier.

"It's too quiet in here, Margie," he hollered into the air. "Just too dang quiet."

Mrs. Spellman's shape filled the bedroom doorway; her head bobbled a nod. "Don't seem right, all this silence."

Max Spellman tossed her a nod. "No, ma'am; don't seem right at all."

# WHEN JESUS LEFT BIRMINGHAM

Some say that once you have the Lord in your life, He won't ever leave you alone. But that can't be all true. I recall a time when Jesus left Birmingham, Alabama. Seems so long ago now, that Sunday morning, like maybe it never happened at all.

But it did.

I can still remember the moment it occurred.

I'd only just turned fourteen the week before. Surely that made me a man, right? In the Jewish religion boys are bar mitzvahed at thirteen, delegating adult responsibilities to the newly proclaimed man. We weren't Jewish, my family and me, but I'd been reading up on these things. That, and the fact that Timmy Horvath, a Jewish boy in my math class, had been given all the rights of a man just a year earlier. Timmy had been bar mitzvahed.

I figured I'd test the moment and see if maybe I could be seen as a man now rather than just a boy.

"Ma," I said, working over the tone of the conversation I was certain would follow my all-important request. "Do you think I could skip church today, maybe stay home with Dad?"

"Get your shoes on, boy," is what she said. "I won't raise a heathen."

"I still believe," I argued. "And I'll still read my Bible. I was just thinking I could—"

"I won't tell you again, boy."

My dad drifted through the kitchen, tossed me a grin on his way to the breakfast table. He didn't believe in God or Jesus or anything that couldn't be seen with his own two eyes. The only time I could recall seeing him in a church was when my Uncle Delbert died in a car crash and they had the funeral at Birmingham Baptist.

"Once you're eighteen," my dad said, "you can do what you want. Until then, you best listen to your mama."

"Timmy Harvath was bar mitzvahed," I explained. "His folks treat him like a grown man."

"We're not Jewish," my dad said, stuffing a strip of bacon into his mouth.

The suddenness of the boom is what startled me the most. The rumble that followed threatened to shake the windows of our house to shards.

My mother let out a "Dear Jesus! What was *that?*"

Janie, my little sister, bolted from her room, panic-stricken and bound for tears. "Is it the Russians?" she cried.

A blur of bodies traipsed past our house, destined for the corner at the top of our street.

A column of black smoke reached for the sky in the distance.

"Keep the kids inside, Madeline," my dad said, stepping into his battered work boots.

I can't say for sure what it was, that notion that shoved me forward, put me in my father's line of vision. His eyes fixed on me; a moment's hesitation drifted between us before he dropped a nod.

I followed him through the front door, across our lawn, and into the street with all the other men from our neighborhood. Urgency filled the air with a thick acrid smell.

We blended in with the crowd gathered at the corner. Voices made claims of this or that being the culprit in the disruption of our morning routines. Truth is, nobody on that corner knew for sure what had happened.

"Let's take a walk down further," my dad said, leading the way toward Sixteenth Street.

Others stayed back, preferring to remain grounded on our own street, as if venturing too far away just might put them at risk of some as-yet understood force.

Ronnie Dooley tore past us on his bike, offering nothing by way of explanation of what he might have seen closer to the source of all that smoke.

My dad's quick steps lost something off their pace the nearer we came to the moment that would forever change the both of us.

We saw it at the same time, that hole in the back of the church building up on Sixteenth Street.

The coloreds' church.

Baptist by denomination—same as us. But white Baptists and black Baptists don't ever mingle on Sunday mornings.

"Dynamite," a man claimed, moving away from the scene.

My dad said, "Let's get on home, son."

I didn't think to argue with him, to challenge his idea to leave the chaos to the authorities. I just followed him back, the both of us walking in a slow silence.

*   *   *

Anguished faces crowded the screen of our Philco television set all that night. Black faces, mostly; those belonging to the men and women digging through what remained of their place of worship.

Twenty-two met with injuries.

Four lives were lost.

Just four little girls, they were; those of an age where they'd giggle at boys making eyes at them.

The man on the television read their names as if telling the score of a baseball game. "Addie Mae Collins, age fourteen; Carole Robertson, age fourteen; Cynthia Wesley, age fourteen; Denise McNair, age eleven."

"The work of the Devil," my mother proclaimed. "Those babies should always be safe in the Lord's house."

Even my father, who'd never really shown a fondness for the colored race, lost tears that day. Those girls were my age, he said. There'd be families missing pieces that night, and what would he do if he sat down to dinner and found an empty place at *his* table?

"I'd surely die without my kids," he whispered to my mother, the words thick in his throat.

My sister spoke the question I'd been pondering from the moment we learned the truth.

"Why didn't God stop those men from doing this?" she asked.

My mother stammered a few words meant to soothe her youngest child.

But words of my own found my tongue pliable to the accusation they meant to administer. "It's because Jesus left Birmingham today. He left those people when they needed Him most."

Terror didn't just leave its mark on the black folks of Birmingham that Sunday morning. Faith of a fourteen-year-old white boy suffered as well. I won't say I quit believing in God and the salvation of Jesus Christ; but how do we live our lives not knowing if He'll protect us or if He'll look the other way?

It's what they call collateral damage in the modern world, those unexpected casualties during an act of terror.

I don't believe I was the only one, either.

# THE DISTANCE

It starts with that gnawing feeling, like a rat trying to chew its way through my stomach, making a meal of my guts as it escapes. I can always tell when a moment is about to turn dark and sordid. Usually, though, it has to do with too much drink, a word said in jest, feelings getting hurt, and a punch is thrown to alleviate said wounded feelings.

A fight? I can handle that.

Todd Colvin's the one who pulled me off the line, putting Kenny Grimes in my place, telling me only that Mr. Tripp needed to see me in the front office.

The front office.

Personal request from Norman Tripp himself.

I expected a reprimand for some dereliction of duty, maybe even a layoff notice—which seemed likely, with the downturn in the economy. People just weren't buying boats the way they once did.

But this had nothing to do with duties being overlooked or fat getting trimmed by way of a layoff.

Tripp's eye drooped in a way suggesting avoidance. "You need to call your mother," he said.

Surreal, I guess I'd call it, being in the big boss's office, being told to call my mother.

I skipped formalities, said, "What for?"

Tripp just nodded toward the phone on the oversized desk meant to match an oversized ego. That's why nobody in the plant liked this guy.

"There's been a death," he said, refusing to make eye contact.

That gnawing, it just wouldn't let up. The rat proved determined to flee the scene as quickly as possible.

"Death?" I said, tasting those acrid letters on my tongue. "Who died?" Stalling tactics, sure; but I really didn't want to make the call.

Tripp, coward that he is, just flinched a shrug. He knew already; knew it before I did.

For that, I wanted to punch him in the mouth.

The phone came heavy to my hand, like just maybe this was all a well-played joke, the receiver having been filled with lead or some other weighty substance. There'd even be a hidden camera capturing my surprised response.

If I'm the one who dialed the number, I don't recall the act.

Mom's voice trembled. "Danny died, Richie. Danny's gone."

My legs buckled; the floor raced up and kissed the side of my head.

My baby brother is no more.

*     *     *

Five years later, that day, that pain, still persists.

It's a hole that can never be filled, leaving an open space where you just know something belongs, a thing that somehow escaped when I wasn't paying attention.

A thing that will never return.

I don't mean my brother as the thing, either. It goes deeper than that. I mean that place in life, of being a brother—*that's* missing. I'm a son now, a father, an ex-husband, a friend, but never again will I be a brother. That's gone, carried away by some force that answers to no man.

Carbon monoxide poisoning. That's the official cause of death. A faulty furnace; a furnace he'd meant to have checked out before fall set in with its cooler nights.

I'd just turned eight when my parents divorced; Danny had been a month shy of four. Neither of us understood this idea of ending a marriage, of splintering a family. Who does that?

Danny became my shadow; he latched on, hoped that the rest of us wouldn't drift too far from him, the way our father vanished. I think that's why I carried around a need to watch over Danny, to protect him, keep him safe from bad things.

I failed, though.

*    *    *

I didn't recognize the woman at the front door. Her type didn't reside in my neighborhood. By type I mean classy, well-dressed, perfect hair, manicured nails—the kind who's married to money and wouldn't do anything stupid enough to jeopardize her good fortune.

"Richard Metzger?" She said it as if she couldn't believe a mother might actually call her child by such a name.

I tipped a nod, shot a glance beyond her, searched the street for her vehicle, for signs of trouble. It's that gnawing feeling that had me on edge. It always portends to something dark, some ominous piece of bad news, a thing I'm never quite expecting.

Her features called to mind a woman who grew up needy—emotionally and physically. Soft, yet jaded; unsure of herself or her place in the world.

"How long have you lived here?" she asked, brushing loose strands of blond hair from her cheek. Thirty, I'd guess; petite; certainly not a drinker or a smoker. She tacked on an afterthought. "If you don't mind my asking, I mean."

"I don't own the place," I explained, "so whatever you're selling, you'll have to take it up with the landlord."

A shake of her head sent us down another road. "My son, he's, well, I don't know how to explain this without sounding crazy." Her laugh came tight, stiff, the sort of laugh that reads forced.

A longer scan of her face found nothing familiar, no recollections of a possible previous encounter, of a night that might have produced another life.

"I can't help you." They were the first words I found in my mouth. "I mean, are you looking for something specific? What is it you expect from me? Child support?"

If I'd had three heads she couldn't have looked at me with greater surprise. "Are you out of your mind?" she hissed. She backed off my front porch, set her black flats onto the cement walk, and eyed me like maybe she'd entertained notions of killing me there on the spot. "My son has memories, of things he's never done, of instances from long before he came into this world. Things you might very well verify. But if you're so arrogant as to think…"

She never did finish her tirade that day.

A week later, though, that's when the rat began eating at my guts again.

*    *    *

"He's got stories," she explained, seated in my kitchen. "These aren't the simple tales of a child, either." She set her elbows on the table, leaned closer, as if the two of us had agreed on some sort of conspiracy. "He tells of how you and him used to pin towels around your necks, how you'd be Batman and he'd always have to be Robin—since he's the younger."

I pulled a sip from my coffee cup. "Kids have been doing that since the first comic books came out. Maybe he saw other boys playing and wanted to be part of it."

The woman would not be denied. "How would he know your name, your address, or that you've lived here for ten years?"

That didn't mean a thing, I told myself. "Anything about me or anybody else can probably be found on the internet." I think I said it as much for me as her.

"He's five years old, Mr.Metzger. He can't even read yet."

"Then maybe you're the one feeding him stories."

"Why? Why would I do that?"

My shoulders sloughed off a shrug. "Why do Nigerians practice their scams on the internet?" I answered the question myself. "Because they're driven by greed. Same as you. I'm not giving you one dime, lady."

"You cut your head open when you were twelve. The doctor had to shave the area to get the stitches in—seven stitches—and your brother took to calling you *Patch*." She said it as if she'd been there, had maybe lived in the neighborhood back then.

"Do you know me?" I asked. "Did you live on my street? What's your angle? I mean, do I have to call the police?" Emotion sparked angry fires inside my chest, had me sifting for better things to say. "Why would you pick at *that* scab? My brother's *gone*, lady!"

Her defense came hurried, frantic almost. "I'm just trying to find answers for my son."

My fingers gripped her arm. It didn't take much force to eject her from my home. "Find another victim, lady," I said, slamming the door on the very idea.

*     *     *

"Go to the police," my mother said, "get one of those restraining orders, keep her away from you."

I dropped onto the sofa in her new apartment, pondered a thought or two. I asked, "Do you remember when I cut my head open?"

Mom said, "Seven stitches, if I recollect."

"Do you remember what Danny started calling me?"

A smile played on her lips, as if a long-neglected memory suddenly showed itself alive and well. "Patch," she said, nearly whispering the word. "And you'd get so angry—but you were always so quick to forgive him."

"She knew about Patch and the seven stitches—her *son* knew, I mean." I shifted on the sofa, stared blankly at the photograph of me and Danny, aged eighteen and fourteen, taken during the summer of 1985. "Maybe I should meet this boy, at least hear him out."

Mom grew adamant. "There is no such thing as reincarnation, Richie.

That's not *Christian!*"

I never mentioned that word myself—though the concept did lurk just outside the periphery of my mind. I could feel it there, staring, stalking, daring me to take hold and examine such a notion.

"I know, Mom," I said, gaining my feet. "It's not Christian."

*     *     *

"Suppose you tell me a few things," I said, eyeing the blond-headed boy with suspicion. I shifted in my seat, uncomfortable with this whole notion his mother intended to drop in my lap. It had to be the mother's idea; boys his age aren't capable of such scams. "Tell me something nobody but Danny and I know about."

We sat in a corner booth at Pelligrino's Diner—a place Danny never visited. Danny hated Itailian food. Tomatoes made him sick; didn't matter if they were raw, stewed, or turned into sauce. Weird kid—wouldn't even eat *pizza!*

Blue eyes gawked at me, as if the kid meant to memorize every line in my face; his shy stare gave away nothing showing familiarity.

The woman, the ringleader in this charade, gave her charge a nudge, whispered a thing in his ear.

His voice came low, hushed, as if afraid of being heard. "I don't like it here," he said.

I seized the moment, meaning to intimidate him into folding, to copping to the lie they sought to conceal. "Why don't you like it here? What's wrong with this place? They've got great food." That's when I pulled out the ace. "Are you hungry? You want a plate of spaghetti? The sauce is the best in town."

The boy's head tipped a nod.

Ten minutes. That's all the time it took for that plate to be put in front of him, for this little boy to shovel noodles and tomato sauce into his mouth—a thing Danny would be mortified to do.

I said nothing, though; kept the facts to myself, I did.

"What's your name, son," I asked, watching the tiny kid make short work of Pelligrino's best.

Sauce dripped from his chin, spotted his clean white shirt. "Toby," he said, glancing at his mother, as if searching for the correct answer.

"Your mom says you're Danny."

He dispensed a smile, allowed the woman to wipe his face, said, "I used to be Danny—until that day."

I don't know why but the kid made me uncomfortable. "What day are you talking about?" I asked.

"The day the poison made me die."

"Poison? What poison is that, Toby."

"The kind from the heater."

It was in the newspaper. The local TV news ran a story on Danny's misfortune, a warning to get your furnace checked each year.

"But now I'm just Toby," he explained. "That's how come I like tomatoes now."

*   *   *

"Who's that?" My finger pointed toward the framed photo of a young girl occupying space on my living room wall.

Toby gave up a childish shrug.

"Don't know?" I said it with a harshness I'd never imagined using against a little boy. "You should know her name without any hesitation."

He moved in closer, studied the grainy black and white image as if seeing it for the very first time. "I don't remember her," is what he said.

The mother spoke up, asked, "Who is she?"

I refused to give that away, though. It's something I possessed and he didn't. We knew all about our great-grandmother, Danny and I did. She'd been a famous jazz singer way back in the twenties and thirties. We even stayed with her, back when she lived on Park Avenue in New York City.

Spent a whole month with her in 1975 while our parents fought over who'd get what in the divorce.

"Danny would remember her," I told nobody in particular. "It was the greatest summer of our childhood."

Toby's head bobbled a nod; the words fell from his mouth in rushed excitement. "That big apartment with all those things from the olden days!"

He got that part right, but I still wasn't convinced. "Who is she then?" I asked again.

Another shy shrug, is all the boy managed. He knew nothing of her name, her relationship to me, or of her once-high station in this world. He had bits and pieces—certainly not enough to be Danny.

But still, facts came to light:

Toby had been born on May 3, 2008, the same day Danny died.

Toby recalled the name of Danny's kindergarten teacher without hesitation.

Toby described the stuffed giraffe Danny clung to every night until sixth grade.

And yet he didn't know the name of the street we lived on before the divorce, couldn't recall my daughter's cat's name—a cat Danny bought for her—and had no recollection of Angie Beckham, our babysitter from 1976 until 1978, a teenage girl who, on more than one occasion, showed us her breasts.

Who forgets a memory like that?

"You've done your homework," I said to the mother. "But it's not enough to convince me of anything."

I meant to angle them toward the door, to send them on their way; but the boy, this kid Toby, the one claiming to be my baby brother come back from the dead, pulled away, broke for the corner like he'd been sent there for punishment, and closed his eyes as if in prayer.

"Mr. Morgan," he said, his voice strong and sure. "Remember what I told you about Mr. Morgan?"

*     *     *

Toby referred to that slipping of memory as "the distance." He sounded more a man than child. It just happens, he claimed, that forgetfulness that creeps in as he grows older. Things remembered yesterday are lost fragments today; tomorrow, they'd be dust.

I don't believe in reincarnation—even after the details Toby presented concerning Danny's mid-afternoon stumble into our parents room just before our father moved out. He knew all about seeing Mr. Morgan, the manager from the bank where my mother worked, in bed with mom. He told me about it the day it happened. But I didn't want to hear it. I swore Danny to secrecy, made him promise he'd never tell another soul.

Danny's word held fast.

There were only two people outside of the guilty couple who knew about my mother's indiscretion from all those years ago. One is dead and buried in Mount Carmel Cemetery.

As I said, I don't believe in souls changing bodies. But I can't deny this kid, either. He's got Danny's memories—though they fade in content with each passing day.

The distance.

I promised the boy I'd be here for him, ready to listen as he recalls this moment or that one, recollects some generic summer day I'd long forgotten. He'd lost interest in sharing, though. Maybe he just wanted to get it all out before settling into a childhood of his own.

Is there something to this reincarnation idea, or has my chain just been yanked? I can't say for sure either way. The only notion I *am* certain of is this: we'll all find out for ourselves one day. As Jim Morrison once sang: No one here gets out alive.

# Night Flight

It's just past dinner, right about when the sun gets that lazy way of hanging lower in the sky, when I spy that green pickup truck making a turn onto Clifton Street two blocks up. It could be him. Might only be Mr. Nortak, though. Both of their trucks may as well be twins.

My backside rises from the rickety wooden steps on the front stoop, and I try real hard to draw the distance closer to me.

The truck whips into the Nortak driveway.

It's not him—yet.

Grandma Boyle hollers from just inside the front door, "Come inside, Ray Tom. He ain't coming."

An anxious shuffle has a go at my feet. Nerves have me clearing my throat, testing my voice to see if I can say what's on my mind. "He'll be here soon enough," I manage, though it doesn't come out overly confident. "He just gets hung up sometimes, is all."

"Hung up in that *beer garden*." Grandma says it like she knows for certain.

"You don't know that," I tell her, just as sure of my own proclamation as she is of her own.

Grandma won't give up, though. "Known him longer than you have, boy. He ain't never going to change."

I come off the front stoop, eye that brown grocery sack filled with the clothes I'm meant to wear over the weekend. "Suppose he *does* change? You going to tell him you're sorry for always doubting him?"

Grandma declines a reply this time, letting her silence do all the arguing she's not up to doing herself.

Uncle Verl, baby brother to my mother, lands beside me on the stoop, like he just fell from the evening sky. "Don't pay her no mind, Ray Tom," he says, patting his shirt pocket in a search for that pack of cigarettes that never goes anywhere without him. "She's seeing *my* daddy when she's talking about *yours*."

Uncle Verl, he's a tall, skinny type; wears his brown hair long in back but short on top. He's only twenty-one years old, which is just eleven years older than me. But he doesn't talk down to me like I'm a stupid kid, though.

"Maybe he had to work over again," I say, not truly believing it myself—and *I'm* the one saying it.

"Could be," Uncle Verl says, tucking a Marlboro between his lips. That shiny silver Zippo of his catches the last of the sun, splashes a glare in my eyes. "I'm guessing if he *is* working over, well, you might have to wait till tomorrow to see him. Which means we can have us a go at some of those new Xbox games I picked up on the cheap from Darryl at work."

My shoulders give up that stupid shrug they always do when I can't think of something to say.

"Darryl," I finally manage. "Isn't he the crackhead?"

"Meth," says Verl, "—same difference, though."

"How come he's always selling stuff he only just bought? I mean, that makes no sense to me."

"Yup. But hey, as long as he's cutting *me* a deal, I don't care *what* he does with what's his."

My gaze trips over my grocery sack again. Thoughts of my father tumble through my head, recalling the last two weekends he'd been meant to pick me up, only to have forgotten. He drinks some—just not as much as Grandma Boyle claims.

Verl pulls on his cigarette, breathes off a thick silver-gray cloud that stinks up the air. "Just remember these days," he says, "—when you got kids of your own, I mean." He finds his feet again and wanders down the street toward Tammy Sistler's place.

Tammy's his girlfriend. They have a daughter named Ivy together. Ivy's just six—which means Uncle Verl had only seen fifteen birthdays himself before he became someone's dad. Grandma Boyle doesn't believe for a red-hot minute that Ivy belongs to her Verl.

Grandma just thinks she knows everything.

Me and Mom, we moved in with Grandma Boyle two years ago, once the divorce became final and our old house was sold. It didn't seem fair, me not having a say in where I should live. I mean, Mom's got Grandma and Uncle Verl and Ivy. My Dad's got nobody to come home to after work.

"I'll never get married," I tell myself from time to time. I mean, why do something that will probably just end in a bad way? It always does. Mom and Dad, Grandma and Grandpa Boyle.

Just about every kid at school has divorced parents.

Grandma Boyle snatches up that grocery sack once the sun is completely down behind the trees across the street—which means it's been decided I won't be waiting for Dad anymore tonight.

"Go on out and play while there's a little light left, boy," she says, leaving me alone on the stoop.

It's Chad Nortak that's caught my attention, the way he's standing on the corner where Clifton Street crosses Waycroft Avenue. He's waiting for the others—no doubt looking for a night of trouble. That's what they do, Chad Nortak and Tanner Felcher and Mickey Denby; they break windows, tag buildings with spray paint, and steal from cars left unlocked in the grocery store parking lot. Those boys have seen the backseats of more police cars than most adults. And they're only two grades ahead of me.

"What are you looking at, geek?" Chad hollers in my direction. The boy works over a cigarette like it's the last one he'll ever smoke. "Thought you were supposed to be at your dad's this weekend."

I slough off a shrug, leave it at that.

But Chad, he's the one always looking for the last word in a situation. "Drunk again, is he?"

It's like my middle finger just does its own thing, the way it stands alone, aimed in Chad's direction. "Fuck you," is what I say, loud enough to be heard by him—and by Grandma Boyle!

*"Raymond Thomas!"* Her voice is high and screechy, painful, like tin foil on a cavity filling. "If I *ever*—"

I already know the whole spiel, the threats of soap in my mouth, of weeks on end spent weeding the flower bed along the side of the house.

Chad's laughter pokes holes in the dying light. "Don't take it so hard, geek; my old man's a drunk, too. He's doing a stretch over in county for running a stop sign and wrecking a cop car."

It's my feet that take up that unspoken dare, carrying me to the sidewalk, bringing me closer to the boy known for beating up kids for no particular reason at all. I won't run, though, like those other kids do; I'll stand my ground and fight back. It's a notion I tell *myself*, though I'm having trouble believing it.

Chad's cigarette slips free from his fingers; it's a natural thing, the way he grinds it into the sidewalk under his Nike high-tops.

I say, "I heard you stole those from Jimmy Rickman." I mean those shoes, of course.

I'd never noticed just how dark Chad's eyes could dim once he set his gaze on a particular target.

"Don't be an asshole," is all he says.

"If your dad's in jail," I ask, hoping he won't suddenly sock me for being so nosy, "who was driving his truck earlier?"

"Maybe it was me," says Chad. "Ain't a hard thing, driving a truck."

"You're just twelve, though. Don't the cops stop you?"

"If you drive careful, nobody notices." He sifts his shirt pocket, retrieves another cigarette, tucks it between his lips, just the way Uncle Verl does. "Besides, I'm thirteen, not twelve."

I don't know that I'd call it bravery, but I sure don't feel too scared to ask the question I find in my mouth. "If you're thirteen, then why are you only in seventh grade?"

That dark gaze threatens to grab hold of my throat and strangle the stupid right out of me. But that's not what Chad does. He just spits on the sidewalk, right where everybody has to walk, and mumbles something about being held back last year. Which for the likes of Chad Nortak, that means he flunked.

But Chad, he's not up to discussing his scholarly failings. He dips the tip of his Marlboro into the orange tongue of a pink Bic lighter, sucks the smoke into his lungs, and says, "You wanna tag the high school with us tonight?"

*     *     *

It's an easy enough thing, sneaking out at night. My bedroom at Grandma Boyle's house is just off the kitchen—where the pantry used to be. Everybody else sleeps upstairs. Except Uncle Verl. Most nights he just stays over at Tammy Sistler's place, along with Ivy. When he *does* stay at home he usually sleeps on the couch.

Mom's got his old room. It was hers anyway, back before she met Dad and ran off to Vegas to get married without anybody else even knowing.

They didn't run off to Vegas for the divorce.

My feet feel strange being in shoes at one in the morning. I guess they're just not used to being needed this late at night.

The back door screeches like it means to snitch on me. But nobody wakes up; Uncle Verl sometimes comes in this way when he and Tammy are arguing. I'm the only one who ever hears him, though.

I'd never snitch.

"You ever tag before?" Chad Nortak's words flutter through the air like fireflies going in different directions.

My head floats with excitement, with the rush of being out in the night without anybody else even knowing. Shadows move through Grandma Boyle's backyard, hiding behind those ancient oak trees along the fence line.

What if somebody sees me, decides to tell Grandma?

Chad knocks a hole in the moment, says, "Can't tag with me if you go chicken, geek."

He goes over the fence at the rear of the yard, the loose clang of spray-paint cans in his backpack disturbing the night.

I could just run back inside and avoid the trouble.

But I don't.

Why chicken out now?

My feet slap the hard dirt in the field between our neighborhood and Wendell High School, carrying me quickly toward Chad and his paint cans.

Chad says, "Glad you could make it, geek."

Sweat runs down my spine as if I sprung a leak at the back of my neck. I pull down a few deep breaths, sucking on the humid air, but there's really no way to settle my heart, to keep it from punching its way out of my chest.

I give my voice a try. "Where's Tanner and Mickey? How come they aren't coming along?"

"Because they're mama's boys. They ain't allowed to hang around me anymore." He says it like he means to make fun of those other two, but even tough Chad Nortak can't hide the sad sound of his own voice. "That makes *you* my new accomplice, geek."

Behind Wendell High School it's quiet and dark, so completely still, like maybe God isn't bothering with that particular piece of Earth.

"A blank canvas," says Chad, eyeing those clean bricks. "I do my best work on new walls."

They aren't really *new* anymore, these walls. They've stood for nearly five years.

"Surprised you haven't marked it up by now," I say, amazed at the sound of my own voice. It's somehow deeper than usual, certain, confident.

Chad says, "This one took some planning."

"It doesn't seem like much planning to me. I mean, we just walked up to it without any trouble."

"I'm talking about planning the *work*, geek. A canvas like this deserves only a masterpiece." Chad drops his backpack on the ground, yanks at the zipper, retrieves half a dozen colors for his palette.

I reach for the can of black, eager to spray a cuss word across the brick façade.

But Chad, he's got other ideas. "You never did answer my question from earlier," he says, snatching the can from my hand. "Have you ever tagged before?"

I haven't.

And somebody like Chad Nortak already knows this.

He asks, "Have you ever heard of Jean Michel Basquiat?"

A flinch of my shoulders opens class on an art lesson I don't think I'd ever expected from the likes of Chad Nortak. He tells all about this guy in New York City who went from painting graffiti on buildings to having showings in actual art galleries.

"People paid thousands of dollars for his work," Chad explains, taking hold of a can of blue. The hiss of spray-paint fills the quiet space. "That's what I want to do—except the part where he died of drugs."

We fall into a quiet movement; Chad lays colors to the wall, while I hand him what he needs, always keeping my eyes open for intruders who may not appreciate art.

A scarce light trickles out of the windows closest to that side of the building, offering only a subtle splash of illumination, just enough to know the scene developing is tropical, warm, maybe Hawaiian.

"Tahiti," Chad clarifies, "—where Paul Gauguin painted *his* master-piece."

I can't say for sure exactly how long we've been at this—an hour, maybe two—but the work on the wall becomes something so vivid, so real, like all it would take is to step forward and you'd be there, in Tahiti, on that beach, with that dark girl showing us her boobs.

"How'd you learn to paint like this?" I ask, stunned by the sight, amazed at how quick it came into being.

Chad, his fingers sticky with paint, fishes a pack of Marlboros from his pocket, slips one between his lips, all the while never once taking his eyes off his work. "My mom painted," he says, flicking that pink Bic. Sadness like black ink stains his tone. "I guess I got it from her. She's the one who taught me all about art and those who create it."

His mother had died, though, back before Mom and I moved in with Grandma Boyle.

"How'd she die?" I dared ask.

For a moment that dark gaze of his fixes me hard, like just maybe he's deciding where to hit me the hardest. (Stomach or face?)

But he doesn't punch me. He just tells me all about the cancer treatments that stole his mother's hair, her health, and her life.

"She'd been fine until the chemo," he says, exhaling a silver cloud of smoke. "My dad, he never used to get drunk—not while *she* was around."

At least I still have *my* mom, I think, and my dad—even if he doesn't show up when he's supposed to.

Light bright as a noonday sun suddenly falls directly upon us, as if its source just knew we were there the entire time.

*"Police helicopter!"* Chad yells, bolting toward the field between the school and our neighborhood, leaving me behind with the evidence.

I want to run, too, but my stupid legs won't budge.

*Where's the sound?* I wonder, sifting silence for the noise a helicopter ought to make.

That light, it becomes a solid thing, reaching down from its source, grabbing hold on Chad out in the middle of the field, yanking the boy up into the air, high above the Earth, over the tops of those ancient oaks.

Then it's gone, that strange and silent light.

And gone, too, is Chad.

*     *     *

Uncle Verl's the one who catches me coming in just as the sun peeks over the tops of the trees where I'd last seen Chad Nortak. He won't snitch on me, though, Uncle Verl; not to Mom, not to Grandma. And I can't even tell him what happened when he asks where I've been and how come I look *spooked*.

All I can do is watch TV, search for reports of a UFO or whatever it is was, of sworn testimonies from other people who saw what I saw, of mention of a boy gone missing from our neighborhood.

But who is there, besides me, to report that missing boy?

Who is there to even care?

I'd never snitch.

# MEDAL DETECTOR

Ancient nails and an old horseshoe or two, that's all the earth saw fit to yield thus far. Still, with each crazy squeal emanating from his metal detector, Chance Zamler allowed yet another wild scenario to creep into his head. Maybe there'd be gold coins next time, he imagined, putting a shine on his thoughts. Or possibly, he'd stumble upon some discarded relic from a previously undiscovered tribe gone extinct long before white men ever reached these parts.

The house itself dated to a time around 1820 or so. But the land—who besides the Almighty Himself could untangle such a long and complicated history?

Chance waved that detector side to side in a far corner of the back yard, out where an outhouse once may have stood. It's not at all uncommon to reap treasures from the hidden remnants found beneath old privies—glass bottles, usually—the sorts of items not likely to trip a metal detector. But hey, the guy on the History Channel dug up a genuine brass belt buckle that brought him an easy hundred bucks. The theory being, the Civil War piece ended up in the hole when some drunken Union soldier stepped in to relieve himself.

Chance had uncovered lost car keys before, and a pretty nice World Series ring. But that had been on a beach over near Chesapeake Bay. And the ring, it wasn't even a champion's reward; it belonged to an equipment manager from the losing side of the 1969 fall classic. Even so, it still put three-hundred dollars in his pocket. And just how had it ended up buried in the sand on a Maryland beach anyway? He often wondered. Maybe its rightful owner wore his prize to prove he'd been part of something almost special, a near-miss moment.

Mystery this time came in the guise of an insignificant rise in the earth where his wife intended to sow her garden. Chance's side-to-side wave condensed into shorter movements, a circular focus meant to fix in on whatever lay hidden away beneath that dirt mound.

The detector's chirp issued strong, insistent, like the determined warning of an oriole bent on protecting its nest.

Chance's pleadings came tucked beneath his breath. "Not another nail, please."

But neither nails nor horseshoes stirred the detector the way this latest find had managed.

The spade came to his eager hand. Hard soil fought against his intrusion. Secrets buried two feet under now caught hold on the afternoon sun; gold sparkled in the light.

Chance's voice rose high. "Honey," he hollered. "Come see what I found!"

*     *     *

"How do you suppose they ended up in the ground?" Anna Zamler asked from across the table.

Chance wagged his head. "Doesn't make sense. They weren't in a box or anything. It's like someone just dumped them in that hole and covered 'em up."

But why do a thing like that to something so personal?

He took up the Purple Heart, traced its smooth contours with the tips of his fingers. "This one means he'd been wounded in battle," he explained, "—or maybe even killed."

The engraving on its back whispered a name: James K. Ralston. And a date still remained; Nov. 10, 1918.

Anna moved closer to her husband. "That's the day before the armistice ending the First World War," she said, recalling an answer on some history quiz from a few years back.

Chance met her gaze. "You'd think his next of kin would cherish such things, pass 'em down to later generations, keep 'em in a safe place."

Anna's soft blue eyes found focus on some far-off time when neither she nor Chance would remain to dictate the who and where of their last earthly possessions. "Maybe our great-grandchildren will be better than that."

Altogether, these medals added up to an impressive résumé, spilling details concerning the doings of someone once deemed special. The Bronze Star, for instance, meant heroic or meritorious achievement. A Silver Star signified gallantry in action. And that Medal of Honor—Congress never did just hand those things out like so much Halloween candy.

Anna rose from her seat, retrieved a pitcher of tea from the refrigerator, refilled her glass. "Maybe he once lived here," she suggested.

"I don't think so," said Chance. "There aren't any Ralstons on the land deed—and that goes back well over a hundred years."

"Then how'd they end up buried in our backyard?"

*    *    *

His fingertips trod the keyboard lightly, tapping at all those requisite letters necessary in stringing together this mystery man's name.

"Thank God for Google," said Chance to nobody in particular.

His eyes absorbed the neat lines lying even along the screen, fixing on loose nuggets of information dropped here and there within the vague text, deciphering the random details of a life long gone.

Anna broke from her housework, dipped inside the den for an update. "Any luck?"

"He was born in Syracuse," Chance explained, "—way up in New York. July of eighteen-ninety." He scrolled down into the muck of it all. "Single mother, no father, by the looks of it."

"Scandalous," Anna teased.

A photograph caught the scroll, rode it to center screen.

"That's him!" Chance exclaimed, staring at the grainy image of a doughboy spoiling for a fight. "And he's wearing the medals, too."

Anna dropped low for a better view of the handsome young soldier just home from the war. "Check for next of kin," she said. "You know, brothers or sisters, someone who might still be around."

"He was twenty-eight when he posed for that picture. That was ninety-three years ago. There's nobody surviving him."

But Anna grew adamant. "He might have had kids, which could mean grandchildren. And they may be old, but who's to say they aren't still puttering around in a flower garden somewhere?"

Nothing showed up, though; no mention of sons or daughters, brothers or sisters, could be found among all these indefinite articles that made his life so non-specific.

Anna eyed the text. "There's nothing here about his death, either."

Chance thought it through, gave sound to the ridiculous idea. "Maybe he still is with us." A joke perhaps, but certainly not unheard of. That French woman, the one who died a few years back, had made it to age 121. Chocolate, wine, and a daily cigarette, she claimed, when asked about her secret.

"What if he died here?" Anna suggested. "—In Maryland, I mean. There'd be a death certificate on file somewhere, right?"

Chance reached for the mouse, backed out of the boxed maze belonging to James K. Ralston, and eased into the local public-records site.

A quick scroll through all of Maryland's deceased Ralstons offered nobody named James. Same went for New York state public records; a birth certificate agreed he'd been born into the world, but mention of his having left it somehow didn't exist.

Anna gained her feet, readied a return toward the waiting vacuum cleaner. "Why don't you call your dad," she said, reaching the door. "He knows all about this sort of stuff."

*     *     *

"War is hell, son," said Roger Zamler, eyeing all those hard-earned medals. "That's not just some snappy saying." He'd seen action in the Gulf War, knew all too well the realities of concepts like post-traumatic stress, nightmares, the dysfunctionality of a returned combat vet. "He might've come back completely busted in his head."

Chance gave it some thought, worked on a stray memory of the day his own father returned from war. That look in his dad's eyes, a thing too closely resembling fear—that's an awful heavy burden for a five-year-old boy to have to witness.

Anna cracked the tension right down its center. "Do you suppose he'd been hospitalized?"

Roger Zamler's head drooped, no doubt recalling his own struggles to get back to where he'd once been. "Those boys of the first world war saw some bad times."

Chance offered his own voice. "Maybe there's a psychiatric file on the guy just lying around, collecting dust, waiting for someone like me to sift through it, bring his story to light."

But Roger Zamler wasn't in an agreeing type of mood. "Leave the man buried, son; even ghosts deserve their privacy."

*     *     *

Chance let it fade for most of a week, but those medals, they had a way of yanking him back to the mystery they promised to unravel. The how and why is the part that really gnawed a hole through him. And what exactly became of the recipient of all that hardware?

It just didn't come off a fair deal, allowing a hero to fall among the forgotten. But the internet wouldn't part with any other clues than the meager offerings it already dished up.

But even dead-ends aren't truly without hope.

"Remember that old man?" Chance pondered, seizing on an idea only now taking root. "—The one who kept the lawn mowed all those years this house sat empty."

Anna eyed him over the top of the morning paper. "Sam, you mean? Sam Gruffalo?"

That's the name. He'd carried a fondness for the once-vacant property the way a man might for a woman who could never really belong to him— no matter how long he pined.

Anna folded the paper, pulled a sip from her coffee. "You could give him a call, I suppose—though he does seem a bit senile."

"Eccentric," Chance corrected, "not senile."

*    *    *

The old timer's shelter leaned like a well-oiled lush against a stand of ancient maple trees sipping life from Maryland soil a mile up the road. A pair of spotted bloodhounds hobbled out from beneath a rotted porch to issue warnings they'd never back up in the handful of days remaining on their dockets.

Chance tucked his truck in the spilled shade of a lazy sycamore. Even now he could imagine the old man spinning yarns about receiving his dogs' ancestors way back in the depression, reward for some act of kindness he'd pulled off during a particularly trying moment.

The old man himself appeared like early morning fog, gathered his bones in a neat pile atop a weatherworn rocker hunched lazily on the porch, gave Chance a suspicious once-over.

"Help ya where I can," he promised, "though I ain't at all familiar with that name you mentioned over the phone."

Chance held back at the foot of the steps, offered up all the infor- mation he'd so far unearthed, spoke that Ralston name a handful of times—just in case you know; jog loose a forgotten memory.

The old man shifted in his seat, waited his turn to speak on the matter. "Found 'em buried, huh?" He pondered. "Back of the house, you say?"

Knotted fingers scratched at gray stubble along his jawbone. "Long-ago dead, you ask me."

Chance stole position on that first stair, felt its spoiled wood bow beneath his weight. "But what's his connection to my house?"

Hazy irritation mucked up the old-timer's gaze. "Wanted that house for myself," he lamented. "Shoulda had it, too, if only I had money enough."

Chance dared the second stair—despite that growling pair of hounds. "You're sure you don't recall any stories about a doughboy staying around here?"

A nasty grin split the old man's weathered lips, gave up those hideous gray gums. "Didn't say I ain't heard my share of stories," he proclaimed. "Just said I didn't know that name."

The early thirties, he explained, saw many a strange character wander through these parts. The depression put whole families on the road, chasing after rumors of jobs that scarcely ever existed.

"But if you owned a large enough house," he claimed, "there was money to be made."

Chance took a seat on the top stair, gave ear as the old man spun details on a time that might not even concern the likes of James K. Ralston.

"Ida Simmerly owned your place back then," said the man, "took in boarders from all over the country—hoboes, mostly, freight hoppers just passing through. Not much money in that crowd, though." His shifting weight caused that worn rocker to preach in tongues for a moment. "Then she discovered the pensioners; those wounded war boys got a regular piece from Uncle Sam each month."

Chance stroked the dog nearest to him, as if answers could be found in the smelly beast's oily coat. A pension angle didn't register as plausible. Not for that era, at least. Government money ran scarce in those days. And Chance told the man as much.

But doubt did little to dissuade the old-timer in his telling of tales.

"Wilson promised it," he argued, "and Roosevelt's the one who delivered."

And once Ida Simmerly tasted a regular income, there'd been no chance of retreat from a sure thing.

"She took to a pensioners-only policy in letting out her rooms," the old man continued. "All sorts of doughboys passed through her doors. This Ralston fella, he might've been one of 'em."

Chance tipped a nod, imagined such long-ago scenes played out inside the place he and Anna now called home.

But still, why bury those medals in the back yard?

"Well," the old man pondered, "it might have to do with all those rumors finding life back then."

"What rumors?" Chance wondered.

"The ones claiming Ida—" He dropped the thought, picked up another. "You understand they're just rumors, right?"

Frustration yanked Chance to his feet; his fists took cover inside his jacket pockets. "What rumors?" he demanded.

A weary breath escaped the old man's lips, like life itself had been pulled long-drawn-out from his very core. "Some folks claimed Ida, well, that maybe she wasn't . . . aboveboard in her dealings."

Now they were getting somewhere. Now the truth of the matter would be found out.

Chance regained his seat atop that first step. "She was cheating those boys out of their pay, wasn't she?"

That ancient head wagged left and right. "Cheating 'em, yes—but not the way you're imagining." Those knotted fingers of his fished a tin of tobacco from his shirt pocket, pinched a dip between his cheek and gum. "Word had it Ida had done a few of 'em in. Just the bad-off ones, mind you; those boys who couldn't get around on their own."

Confusion's cloud rained into the moment.

"How'd she make money by killing them?" Chance asked.

"Ida's the one cashed their checks for 'em. Wouldn't be missed, those broken men. Not back then, at least. And those checks kept coming in each month."

A thought collapsed inside Chance's head. "She killed people inside my house?"

"Wasn't ever proven. All they ever got her for was cashing checks of missing men."

Anna wouldn't tolerate it, living in a killer's den. And suppose there was truth to the matter?

Chance cleared his throat, posed the only question that mattered. "Any guesses on where she'd have put the bodies?"

"Leave it be, son," the old-timer implored, pulling his bones upright. "Course if it bothers you that much, I'll be glad to take the place off your hands."

*    *    *

Anna tossed suspicion across the backyard like grass seed, eyeing the lot with determination. "I don't see anything that looks like a grave," she said. "I'll bet he's just trying to scare us, to get us to sell to him real cheap."

"Won't happen," Chance answered her. "Not unless you feel uncomfortable staying here."

Uncertainty crept into her demeanor. She'd worn that look since hearing about Ida Simmerly and those long-ago rumors. "I'm not saying I'm uncomfortable; I just don't like the idea of people getting killed right where we live."

Chance slipped out onto the back deck; his arms went easily around his wife. "Then it stops right now," he proclaimed.

"What does?"

"Searching for answers."

"Doesn't hurt to know," Anna said.

"Sure it does," he told her, pulling her close. "Besides, my dad's right. Even ghosts deserve their privacy."

# FORGET ME (NOT FADE AWAY)

Once a month she makes that three-hour drive just to be near him, her boy, the son of her old age. She always brings a juice box along, a banana, and a copy of his favorite story. It's worn at the spine now, that book. And even though he's heard it a thousand times, she never tires of reading aloud from *Where the Wild Things Are.*

It's all she can afford now, these once-a-month reunions. Maybe someday her situation will ease, burdens might grow lighter. More likely these monthly traipsings will lose all their meaning and fade like most everything else.

That's the worst part, the missing out on what's already been done, forgetting what you know—even the good parts.

She'd just turned forty-six when her body began to change. Menopause, she figured—until the doctor claimed otherwise.

"Pregnant," he said.

"Can't be," she retorted.

"Can so," he assured her.

Twenty years of marriage and twenty years of trying brought only twenty years of failure. She blamed him and he blamed her, and nothing ever got done about it. They couldn't afford any of those fancy fertility clinics with all their expensive fertility drugs. To adopt, well, Ted's drinking put that option to rest.

It came about on a hot August night a full two years after the divorce. Just once, is all it took by then. And Ted, well, he'd been too drunk to recall any particulars of that brief moment.

"Can't be mine," he claimed.

"Can so," she assured him.

He never did live long enough to see the resemblance in his son's face. Cancer got at him, took him down a week too soon.

Ten pounds is awful big for a newborn. But that just meant he was healthy, carried none of the wreckage left in Ted's wake. This one, he'd make his own mess—good or bad.

Arlington, Virginia, lured her down from the highway, sent her along to what still held a certain familiarity—vague, though it had grown.

He'd be waiting for her, like always, out there in the middle of it all. That's just his way, always needing to be the center of attention.

Except for kindergarten.

"I don't wanna go, Ma," he said that first day.

"Nothing to be afraid of," she assured him.

Then that pretty little blond-headed thing traipsed past, those pigtails tied with pink ribbons, and that was that. Nothing could come between those two—until Kandahar, that is.

They joined up together right after graduation. The Mr. and Mrs. they meant to become had to be put on hold. Noble cause, they both agreed; the needs of a nation.

Ted had been of a noble breed once, as well, back when the cause answered to the name of Vietnam. He never really did return from those faraway jungles.

*    *    *

The backpack came easy to her hand, though its weight promised more than just a simple box of juice, a banana, and Sendak's masterwork. Like maybe a secret or two might have stowed away when she wasn't looking. Hard telling, what with the way things fade anymore.

Her feet found solid ground outside of the car. A quick spring breeze swirled around her like a cleansing devil, blowing away winter's heavy sediment. She wouldn't breathe, though—not just yet. Not with the confusion in the air, a thing thick as dust.

"Afghanistan," she said aloud.

"Afghanistan," she repeated.

Speaking that name made it real, brought it all back to the day he first spoke it.

She went first, that little blond-headed thing with the pigtails. An IED, they called it, some sort of explosive device. It went off beside the road just as her vehicle made its pass. If those in charge were to be believed, she never felt a moment's pain.

But how would they know?

Civilized people never sent their daughters into harm's way.

Never.

The contents of her backpack spilled out before that white stone with his name spelled out in bold black. Just twenty-three, is all he'd been. Gone by his own hand, in a tent in that godforsaken patch of earth somewhere over there. He'd received word of her demise, decided the mother he left at home wasn't enough to keep him tethered to this world, swallowed a bullet from his own rifle.

"Suicides go to hell," the priest claimed.

"Where's that written?" she wondered aloud.

Never did get a definitive answer, a particular scripture of any kind. Just a lot of red tape, is all.

"Arlington, sure," said the man in charge. "Just not National."

She pressed the straw into the juice box, set it before his stone, peeled the banana like she did all those years ago.

"How about a story?" she asked, holding that book of imaginary monsters.

It's his face she recalls easiest—though not the one he took when he left. It's the one he wore back when he was just five or so that comes to mind. The ones that came after, they've all faded now, wiped clean by some doctor's pronouncement.

"Alzheimer's," he called it.

"Silly name, that," she said.

"When it's gone, it's gone," he promised.

Can't quit the inevitable. A thing like disease will go where it wants, do what it will, all the while mocking those who bear its destruction.

Even her name slips away from time to time, like a mischievous pup gone for a roam. It always returns, though, jogged by a particular memory, an emotional sentiment more likely fictitious in its resemblance than real. But who is there to remind her?

The banana goes uneaten, the juice box untouched, the same way it always is after each visit. But he heard Sendak's words—of that she can be sure. It's his favorite story, after all. He'd never miss out on a visit from the monsters.

"Give him back," she whispered at that patch of earth.

Pleading is useless, though; the ground never returns what's been buried.

It came to her then, a mind of its own, that heavy black revolver stowed away inside her backpack.

She remembered now, the intent of such a device. It could certainly bring about the end a chapter or two sooner. Maybe they'd be waiting for her, Ted and her boy.

Would he still call her Ma on the other side, or would the crossover change that relationship? And suppose the priest is right?

Could they share a place in hell together?

Cold steel pressed hard against her temple; her finger found rest on the trigger. Maybe swallowing would be the better way to go. That's how he did the deed, her boy.

But intent fell short of action; more so from fear than any fading from disease. She still had that.

Fear.

Fear of living and fear of dying.

It's all the same, though; living is dying. Some just take longer to get around to it.

*    *    *

Once a month she makes that three-hour drive back to her home, away from him, her boy, the son of her old age. The backpack lies empty now, fallow, but for the book. That other thing, heavy with potential, found rest in a trash can inside the park. No sense in keeping damage within arm's reach. Besides, there were tablets of the sleeping sort she could always turn to for that kind of comfort—but only if life ever grew so dire.

And surely it wouldn't.

Not with those other ones always stopping by, checking on her welfare, offering their own brand of comfort.

Family, of some sort. Ted's kin, most likely, with their two youngsters who took to calling her "Grandma" out of habit. And she didn't mind, either. Their boy called to mind her own boy. And their girl, she could pass for that little blond-headed thing—without the pigtails, of course.

Girls today don't do pigtails, claimed the child's mother.

They never did mind her slips—like calling their boy by her boy's name. A thing like that only made them draw closer to her.

"Why don't you come stay with us, Rose?" the man often asked. "Let us look after you for a while."

"Don't need any looking after," she'd assure him.

But truth to tell, she did need help, someone to look after her, to keep it from getting away from her.

Her hand found the telephone where she left it last. Names and numbers never came easy anymore—not like they once did, back when a thought was readily retained.

Maybe they'd call her, she hoped; save on all that random confusion looking for places to grow, to bear fruit of a rotten nature.

Or maybe this, too, would pass, leaving her to her old self once again. Perhaps all those lost thoughts would return, restoring things to the way they'd once been.

"Neat and orderly," she promised herself.

But he wouldn't be there, no matter how clear her thoughts. He'd never come to her again—at least not in this life. And maybe there's the blessing in her disease: the more things fade, the less those losses are felt.

Even, perhaps, the loss of life.

# YEARBOOK

My photograph is there in the yearbook, smack in the center of page 57, right above my full name: Thomas Alvin Rieger, Jr. I hate that picture, though. Not too fond of the name, either. I mean, a fresh haircut never translates into a cool character. And judging by the sparkle in my eyes, I do believe I was stoned that morning.

The name? It's not really mine. It belongs to my dad.

We're nothing alike, him and me.

Anyway, my mom made sure the yearbook committee included my picture when everybody else just wanted to forget. I suppose it's her way of proving I had nothing to do with all the trouble that jumped off right before spring break. I mean, we were set to spend a week in South Beach. Why would I jeopardize a trip like that?

But Tristan and I were best friends; everybody just assumed I shared complicity. Officer Tenneman sure thought so.

Thing is, Tristan never told me.

Not even a hint.

Nothing of that awful morning stands out, no warning signal, nothing spelling evil intent. Subtlety belongs to the cunning, I guess. Besides, I'd have stopped him had I'd known.

But I didn't know.

Can't convince the good people of Thornville, though.

Tristan's mother died of an overdose, he once told me. Heroin, he claimed. But you could never be certain with the likes of Tristan Chalmers; details tended to shift in the retelling of a story. His father? Who knows. Foster families and apathetic relatives played three-card monte with this boy's life. He never had what most people take for granted.

I first met him in an alley behind Sandusky's Party Store, where all the stoners go to get high before school. The air blew crisp that morning, cold enough to lay ice to puddles gathered where the pavement falls in dips. Tristan didn't wear a jacket like everybody else; all he sported was a pair of acid-washed jeans and a faded black Nirvana concert T-shirt.

Tina Yelba spoke to him first, said something like, "Aren't you cold?"

Tristan flinched a quick shake of his shaggy head, said, "Nope," before offering a joint of his own. "Anybody wanna match me?"

My eyes fixed on that pinner. "You call that a joint?" I asked, retrieving a fat one from a half-empty pack of Marlboros. "This, my friend, is a joint. One toke will put you up there with Sputnik."

His dark gaze scanned the clear sky overhead. "I don't think Sputnik's still up there," he mused. "In fact, I'm pretty certain it's not. And neither is Mir."

Tina giggled, ogling the boy with boldness. "Are we gonna smoke, or are we gonna talk Russian space junk?"

We wandered in a quiet high back to school, the three of us, speaking only when comparing notes on just how stoned we actually were.

Tina had a thing for him right away; one of those mad crushes she could never allow herself to have for me—even though I'd known her since kindergarten.

"I see you as a brother," she told me the one time I tried my best move on her.

But hey, that was freshman year. It doesn't really count, right? I mean, nobody expects to score in ninth grade, do they? Everybody brags on such things but seldom is legitimate proof of anything beyond a hickey ever offered—and even those are suspect.

We became fast friends; a tight trio; Tristan, Tina, and me. A lot of weed got smoked; classes were skipped. After the trouble jumped off, everybody blamed Tristan for all of Thornville's problems. Truth is, we were getting high and cutting class long before he ever showed up. And nobody ever thought much about it, either.

Until that Friday.

I wouldn't call Tristan a popular kid at school. But he wasn't bullied, either. He had no real enemies—at least none that I knew of. And I'd like to believe he'd have told me if there'd been problems.

We got high that morning, same as always, out behind Sandusky's. He didn't act differently from any other day.

The thing with Tristan, though, is he never really said a lot—stoned or straight. He lived by the belief that the more people say, the more of themselves they give away, until there's nothing left, no secrets, nothing to call yours alone.

Maybe he'd reached that point—in his own way of thinking, I mean. The guy just never really had anything to call his own. Whatever there might have been, it all went away with his mom.

Mrs. Rainy's art room absorbed the tail end of those first echoes coming from the opposite side of the second-floor hallway.

"Firecrackers," claimed Delvon Marlin, finishing a watercolor meant to be flowers of some sort.

But LeRon Keege heard it in a different sort of way. "Ain't no firecrackers," he argued, moving toward the door. "That's a piece, Dog."

Me? I guess I didn't care either way. I'd gone missing inside my own head, working on a sketch of a girl I'm pretty sure doesn't really exist. I couldn't get her eyes right, though. I'd meant her to be Chinese. Instead, she just appeared sad.

Screaming kids scrambled into the long hallway. Chaos seized custody of the moment like a truancy officer taking charge of some class-cutting freshman.

We all crowded the doorway hoping for a glimpse of reality, of somebody else's nightmare.

Mrs. Rainy's voice ran high and tight. "Get back inside and shut the door!" she demanded.

I saw him, though—Tristan, raising a black pistol level with Mr. McKutchin's head. The sudden report gave me over to a startled flinch, an immediate thing that nailed my eyes closed for only a moment, so I didn't actually see the act itself. The aftermath, though—a mind can't undo the truth.

Behind the locked door of Mrs. Rainy's classroom, spastic kids flung themselves through open windows, dropping two stories down, landing hard against a strip of grass stretched between the building and a parking lot, preferring the prospect of a broken leg or a fractured arm to the pinch of lead passing through gray matter.

I couldn't jump, though—not that I feared the fall. I just figured if anybody could bring Tristan back to his senses, it would have to be me.

Problem is, Tristan had gone MIA in the time it took to convince Mrs. Rainy to unlock the door and let me out.

A stark dark quiet lounged lazily atop Mr. McKutchin's prone body. The scene brought to mind a drunken uncle sleeping away an all-night bender in the very spot he chose to fall. It might have spawned a few laughs—if not for all that blood.

I can't recall too much about the mess inside McKutchin's classroom. I only remember bodies, three or four maybe, slumped over their assigned desks, like napping stoners bored with the day's lesson.

A scuffle overhead provoked another round of firecrackers mingled with the panicked cries from kids caught too high up to just toss themselves to the ground below.

Jennifer Littman burst from the stairwell like a wild-eyed spider monkey, fixed her frantic gaze on me, and hollered, "Why are you guys doing this, Tommy?"

"I'm not!" I yelled at the retreating girl.

Other kids bolted past me, eager for escape, most already working out details for stories they'd offer to the gathering horde of news maggots waiting at the finish line.

I cut against the grain, shoved my way toward the third floor, up to where Tristan's current commotion dug deep into Mrs. Kennerly's typing class. The wounded and the scared plunged into the hallway, searching for a reprieve that wouldn't come easily.

How does one go about unplugging a hard-wired head case?

A thing almost invisible drifted through shadows just past Mr. Ronson's chemistry lab. I knew that shirt, Nirvana, Teen Spirit, and all that noise.

That shaggy head turned my way. He didn't raise his pistol, though; Tristan knew me.

"I give you the day off, Tommy," he said, dipping deeper into the shadows. "Go home, dude."

"Why would you do this?" I wondered aloud.

He never did tell me, though. Tina Yelba tumbled into the scene like an actress who's missed her mark, jumped her cue.

I don't for a moment believe he intentionally meant to shoot her; Tina was practically his girlfriend. I'm of the opinion he mistook her for another girl, raised that piece, squeezed its familiar trigger, before actually considering the facts of the moment.

And he didn't stick around to lament this accident, either. Those shadows covered him like spilled ink on paper.

Tina never moved again. Tristan's bullet settled in her head, right above her left eye, put the girl lifeless and lost on the hallway floor.

I stayed with her for a minute or two, held her hand, pondered that glassy-eyed stare I'd never get out of my own head. I suppose I'd have made it out unscathed had I just remained there with her, or maybe taken Tristan's advice and gone home. But when does a teenager ever consider common sense?

A flash and a pop put Tristan in the stairwell leading back to the second floor—or maybe the first, if he meant to escape.

There'd be no escaping this mess, though.

Officer Tenneman crouched low in the main hallway, shielded behind a book-return box near the library; waiting, stalking, as if he himself entertained intentions of a murderous sort.

I occupied space beside a drinking fountain just inside the west entrance.

Tristan might have stood a chance had I been inclined to issue a courtesy shout. I didn't feel especially inclined, though. He had to answer for all he'd done—specifically for Tina.

The first shot from Tenneman's pistol struck Tristan's shoulder, spun him reckless and wild into the great wide open, where a second bullet tucked itself neatly against the boy's heart.

Tristan's hand betrayed him, loosened its grip, let fall his own gun, brought his brief reign to an end.

It should have been finished right there. But like I said, me and Tristan were best friends; the assumption of my complicity fell across every remaining face in that hallway.

A combat stance, they call it, that aggressive crouch officer Tenneman adopted. Gusto clouded his gaze. He'd waited out a career for this sort of action. He would not be denied.

My hands rose in quick surrender. "I'm not part of this," I swore.

"Sure you are," he declared, squeezing gently his trigger finger.

*     *     *

They never charged him for shooting me—Officer Tenneman, I mean. My death became one of thirteen attached to Tristan Chalmer's rampage. Mrs. Rainy never said a word, even though she saw the entire scene play out from her hiding place in the stairwell.

And I can't admit to being angry about it, either. I mean, Tristan's to blame for stirring up the whole mess. Everybody else—we were just the debris from whatever it is that set him off. And that's something even the experts can't agree on: Why did he do it?

It doesn't really matter, does it? It's not like they'd ever learn enough to see the next one in time to stop it.

Still, my picture's in the yearbook. Tristan's isn't, but mine is, smack in the center of page 57, right above my full name: Thomas Alvin Rieger, Jr. Maybe I don't really mind that photograph. And just maybe my name's not so bad, either.

# Bad Acid At Woodstock

"Holy cow!" Bobby exclaims, peering through our living-room window. "What the hell is that?"

"Bobby!" Mama hollers from the kitchen. "I told you about using that kind of talk! You want I should feed you a bar of soap instead of supper?"

Kenny creeps in and sports a gawk of his own. "Whoa!" he declares. "I heard they fetched four pairs of 'em back from Vietnam in the sixties. I never did believe it, though."

It's vibrating and hopping up and down on our front lawn like it means to menace only our family. Sometimes it even shakes the whole house.

Todd fearfully says, "I didn't think those things were real."

Too short to see out the window, Nicole tries to pull herself up. She whispers to Bobby, "It's not you-know-what, is it?"

"No, Punkin," he assures her. "It ain't that."

It's curiosity that lures Mama to the living-room with a fresh pot of stuff in her hands. Once her good eye tags that thing, though, she drops the pot and stuff goes all over the floor. Her cry sounds something like, "Why's it in our yard?"

"I ain't sure," Bobby replies. "It just keeps on bouncin' and hummin' and vibratin'."

Nicole offers reassurance. "It's almost like you-know-what, Mama, but it's not."

Just then, Moped, a neighborhood dog, approaches and barks at the thing. But the thing is too loud, and we can't hear Moped's bark. We can only see his mouth move.

"Damn!" Bobby yells. "Did y'all see that?"

We all certainly did see it. Poor Moped never stood a chance. All we could do was stand and watch.

I turned my head, unable to view those last few seconds.

"What was that thing grabbed ole Moped?" Kenny wonders aloud.

Mama tells us what she knows. "Hear tell it's called a ligamatrix."

"If it gets too close to the window," Bobby informs us, "my ass is out the back door."

"I once heard you could shoo it away by spraying it with a garden hose," Kenny's remembering, "—but only after it lets down two or three of them reflector thingies."

Todd says, "Might could rust it."

Just then, it bounces smack dab in front of our window. We all jump back. The glass shatters, and we each one of us scampers through the kitchen toward the back door. A ligamatrix creeps in like a wayward snake and snatches the slowest, smallest one of us.

"Oh! It's got Nicole!" Mama cries, shooting a parting gawk over her shoulder.

Bobby hollers, "Somebody grab her!"

Too late. It sucks her into its gaping maw and begins to hum and whirl, just like it did when it got poor ole Moped.

"Hell, I'm just glad it didn't get me," Kenny proclaims outside the back door.

"Yeah," Bobby agrees. "I mean, I like Nicole and all—but hell, better her than us, right?"

"I suppose you boys is right," Mama confirms as we wander back inside our house.

But that thing on our front yard takes to spinning again, awful fast this time. We start for the back again, real quick-like, climbing over each other in our attempted escape.

All of a sudden it stops and stands completely still, like maybe something got broke inside of it. A second maw gapes wide, and vomits the slowest, smallest one of us onto the ground.

Nicole stumbles and staggers, covered in orange ooze that's digested her sunsuit and flip-flops, leaving her naked, dizzy, and laughing.

"That was fun," she giggles.

Mama calls to her. "Well, hurry and get back in here before it grabs ya up again!"

"I wanna go again," Nicole protests, pouting as she stomps into the house.

It's gone bored now—or maybe sour in its belly. All that hopping up and down and vibrating just stops, like a show-off who can't get anybody to pay it any mind.

Finally, the thing folds in upon itself and, when it becomes small as a nickel, flies straight up into the sky, vanishing from our neighborhood.

"Whew!" Bobby says. "I'm sure glad that's over with."

"Gonna have to get that window fixed," Mama complains. "Third time this month."

We all sit round the kitchen table watching Nicole scrape off orange ooze before it takes to digesting her.

"I'm just glad it wasn't you-know-what," she says, sighing.

And I have to agree with her. I'm also glad it wasn't you-know-what.

# Rave On

Ten minutes till.

The clock beside my mattress flings every spent second into my lap, nudging me so much closer to whatever is about to happen. Mom can't be bothered with it; she's passed out in the next room, oblivious to my escape into night. And even though I'm certain I'll be home long before sunlight splits the dark, my body still bristles with something akin to static electricity, a tight anxiety over knowing I'll surely be found out. And it really doesn't matter; I've been caught before.

Shadows engorged with blackness lurk like thugs in the corners of our backyard; delicate dew blankets the grass like the blood of others foolish enough to go before me.

Blood.

That's what it's really all about, isn't it?

Life?

My mind sports with competing scenarios of what I hope might happen and what I pray will not—Lord knows I don't need any more lectures regarding proper behavior for a young lady.

Five minutes till.

What if they don't show? Suppose this is all just a well-played joke, with me as its shiny white butt?

But this is Molly we're talking about—faithful Molly.

Mom's old sneakers swallow my feet in a comforting fit. The back door whines protest against my departure. Nobody steps forward to quash my moment. I'm all alone.

A lustful breeze plays peekaboo with my nightshirt and soothes my heat. I'm bare underneath. That's the part that excites me most: knowing the only thing standing between me and the real world is a thin scrap of white cotton.

The street out front offers neither light nor sound, as if nothing decent dare occupy such a miserable piece of earth but Donnington Trailer Park and the white-trash misfits it spawns. That's what kids at school call me: white trash. That, and Icky Nicky.

My given name is Nicole—Nicole Lynn Robishawl. I can't quite peg the origins of a name like Robishawl, but I'd bet a hundred bucks its roots lie buried someplace in Europe—the far northern part. I own a headful of blond tangles and uncomplicated blue eyes to prove that theory. And there's another of those curious little oddities assholes around here like to whisper about when they're certain I'm not listening: Mom and Dad are both dark-haired and dark-eyed.

Two minutes till.

I reach the crumbling sidewalk and crouch low beside a naked mess of annuals meant to spruce up the front of our trailer. A word like hatred doesn't begin to tell of my feelings for a shithole like Donnington. We aren't even supposed to be here, Mom and me. Dad promised to take us in, giving me back my old room, if only there'd be no more drinking. But mom prefers vodka to a husband.

Lightning spatters a silvery web across the sky right above Lincoln High School, and my silent prayer for a direct hit goes unanswered. Dull rumbles chase the flashes, but even thunder can't match the wicked growl of Tommy Mizvinski's engine.

He's early!

A full sixty seconds early!

My frantic dash launches me recklessly toward the corner at the end of my street. Tommy won't wait. If I'm not there under that lonely streetlight, forget about it. No rave for me.

I'm there before he is, though, quick enough to spy that single head-light slicing open the night—our night. Sweat jogs the course of my spine.

My heart swears an oath to knock a hole through my middle. I've waited all month to have this moment.

Tommy's door yawns wide; his lanky body leans forward, offering me the back seat. "Get in, Sped," he huffs. "They won't wait around if we're late."

Sped. That's short for special ed. Tommy's the only one who calls me that—even though I've never ridden the short bus.

The lure of this moment sucks me in, puts me close to Molly. Our bodies bump in the darkened back seat, tossing up loose sparks of anxiety. Nervous giggles supply our greetings.

I'm the one who suggested we go to this thing. Faithful Molly, she even tried to talk me out of it. And truth be told, I'd have laid odds on her just staying home. But here she sits, dressed like me—only her nightshirt is pink. I hate pink.

Dale Harvitz rides shotgun. That lazy eye of his gets all hung up on me the entire trip—as if I'd even consider the likes of him. Dale is the true sped in this car, not me. But he's also Tommy's best friend, which makes him more welcome on this ride than me, so I won't call him a sped to his zit-covered face.

Still, I'm the one who set this up. "Where are your pajamas?" I ask.

Jeans and T-shirts, that's what both boys are sporting.

Dale's the defensive one. "Fuck that noise," he spits. "I'm not wearing pajamas to a rave."

I produce the flier, wave it in his pizza face. "That's the theme. It says so right here."

"They won't turn us away, Nicole," Dale argues. "They hold raves to make money. I've got my twenty bucks."

Tommy has his say, lays down his own law. It's me and Molly that has him spooked—our ages, that is. "Just don't go acting like a pair of babies," he tells us, "and they'll probably let you two inside."

Dale lights a Marlboro and eyes Moll and me like he's starving and we're medium-rare fresh-off-the-grill. You can just tell his mind is stuck in the muck and sinking fast. "Got twenty bucks says they're both still bald," he wagers.

Call it a natural reflex, that way my knees squeeze together. He'll never know what's what where those sorts of things are concerned.

Tommy, though—he finds me in the rearview, holds my gaze the way I wish he'd hold my hand, before returning to the road ahead. "Thing like that doesn't concern me," is all he says of the matter.

But then he finds me again and goes back to his law. "Either of you girls get pinched," he orders, "don't you dare mention my name. Cops raid these things all the time. If they snatch you, tell 'em you snuck out on your own, let 'em take you home."

I have no intention of getting caught. I've waited too long for a night like this one. If we are among the chosen, well, then it's meant to be; it's already been tossed up to fate. That's called providence or something. Anyway, Tommy's been to half a dozen raves, and none of those were ever raided.

Tommy's one-eyed Cutlass angles hard onto the shoulder, finds that service road leading away from Summitt Highway. You never drive directly to a rave; there's a proper etiquette involved. Besides, they won't let you in if you just show up. Not even for a hundred dollars.

The designated pickup point calls to mind a crop circle at the center of Hatcher Field. A lonely pair of white minivans promise travel to other worlds.

It's the swirling crowd that yanks at my attention, puts me up on the little secret nobody else in the car has deciphered just yet.

"Let us out," I demand, kicking at the back of Tommy's seat. It's mostly guys doing all that swirling, which means girls are the priority to board those vans. And if Tommy catches on, none of us are going.

Pizza-face Dale pops his door open.

Moll and I spill into the night like twist-cap wine from an overturned

Dixie cup. We bolt toward the closest van and ignore Tommy's orders to wait for him and Dale. But they're not coming along with us—at least not on this trip. Any fool with eyes can read a scene like the one we've tumbled into. Moll and I—we'll be welcomed on this go-round. And a ride home, well, what did that matter at this moment?

A black guy spies us, waves us over; he lures me and Moll into a void between those white minivans. I recognize him from school, though I doubt if I could come up with a name to match his face if given a dozen guesses.

Dark eyes roll over Molly first, then me. A grin parts his lips, shows off teeth like fine white porcelain. "Freshmen, huh?" he asks.

Neither Moll nor I acknowledge his question; we both offer him our twenty dollars instead.

"Awful eager, ain't you?" he asks, drifting between us like lazy smoke. "Suppose it ain't money gonna get you on one of them rides? How bad you wanna go?"

I hear Molly's voice before words have a chance to form on my own tongue. "Whatever it takes," she promises.

That's not the Molly I know.

The Molly I know is far too shy to undress even in front of her own shadow.

That dark gaze of his attaches itself to me. "How about you, Robishawl?" he wonders. "How far are you willing to go?"

Hesitation nearly steals my words—but only for a moment. "I'm with Molly," I inform him. Just leave it open, let him interpret the meaning.

His grin softens into a familiar thing—almost friendly. "Go on and get in line for communion," he says.

Communion?

I'm not even Catholic.

And neither is Molly.

The black guy snatches our money, straps red bracelets around our right wrists, and warns against us taking them off for any reason at all. "That's the only thing gonna get you inside once you get there."

This is the part I love most about raves: all that secrecy, the feeling of being someone special, a chosen one.

Moll and I join a small congregation behind those vans, out of sight of Tommy and Dale and every other guy getting left back tonight.

"Kneel for the rites," orders a skinny white guy sporting stringy black hair down to his shoulders.

The grass, wet with dew, is cool beneath my knees. My head tips back, my mouth falls open, awaiting the chemical sacraments about to be administered.

"Ecstasy," says our high priest, placing a tablet on my tongue.

I swallow before I can chicken out.

Moll swallows too.

Midnight's moon splits the clouds just for a moment; it's large and swollen, shiny as a new dime.

Molly's lips brush against my ear. "Are you gonna, you know . . . ?" she whispers. Bubblegum-sweetened breath warms my neck.

"I have to do it," I assure her. "I'm gone past due."

"We can't have that," she says, snatching hold on my hand, yanking me into the van.

*     *     *

The pull of freedom lures us an hour south of town, out where the old Piven Industrial Park crouches low among tangled weeds and ancient willows long past weeping, forgotten by all but a few hundred ravers.

The van door slides a wide yawn and, like an overfed bulimic, vomits us in front of the warehouse. Familiarity like a scent fills my head. I know some of them, these other girls; upper-class types, mostly; the very sort who'd normally call me Icky Nicky.

But not tonight.

Tonight, everybody's equal.

Molly's the eager one. Those small hands of hers clasp my shoulders from behind; she gives me a push inside the oversized building, into a swirl of underdressed boys and girls bumping and rubbing against a thumping beat intent on recalibrating my heart's natural rhythm.

Lights of yellow and red, blue and green, flash from above like stalking nymphs bent on finding us out.

I pull Molly closer. "Find the water station," I yell over the din. "Keep hydrated."

That smile of hers—that's what makes her Molly. "You picked one already?" she hollers, her small body becoming entangled with that steady beat.

A nod bobbles my head; I leave her there at the edge of a makeshift dance floor alive with hope and boys.

Molly likes boys.

A nameless guy hovers near the door, blue eyes clouded over with that familiar euphoria only a thing like Ecstasy can conjure.

"I've been waiting for you," I tell him, mixing promise with potential.

His fingers find his chest, a gesture meant to convey a Who, me? tone. But words fail the boy's lips; he's too far along for conversation.

My hand fits snugly into his. It falls to me to find a private place for us to get through what has to be done. Fine by me; I've been this way before, done this sort of thing innumerable times. But there's never much chase, not like there was when it first started. Back then, well, it was usually the older ones, the perverts, that went for the chase.

"There's a place around back," I tell him, pulling the guy into night.

"I wanna touch your hair," he says, stumbling behind me like a freak on a leash.

Overhead, the spring sky opens wide, clouds flee, leaving us to our shared intimacy.

Beneath the loading docks is where I take the boy, in full view of a witches' moon—if you're so inclined to believe in such things.

My lips find his; a sneaky gesture meant only to settle any loose nerves.

Clammy, clumsy hands grope me beneath my nightshirt, finding my body bare and eager—maybe even hungry for such a touch. Had this one been in the car with us to take the bet, he'd have easily taken twenty bucks off Dale.

But tonight isn't his night.

A quick nip with my incisors opens the skin just below his jaw, exposing the plump jugular. Barely a flinch, is all he offers. Ecstasy makes our moment easy; there's no room for a fuss.

It's instinctual, that urge pushing me to rip into that purple vein. His salty rush fills my mouth, stirs a familiar frenzy inside my soul. The boy's struggles come cheap, a thing most fraudulent. I hold his body tight against the crumbling concrete, draw long and deep on his life until there's nothing left to take.

They're beautiful when they fade, so pale and blue, like a years-old rose pressed between the pages of a lost lover's book of poems.

*     *     *

Molly is bare beneath her nightshirt. I can tell by the way the pink fabric clings to her sweat-dampened body.

That smile of hers ignites a heated rush through my blood no drug could ever challenge.

"Did you drink any water?" I holler, stepping between her and the Asian kid she's dancing with.

That's the thing with Ecstasy: it'll keep a person moving for hours, without a thought toward maintaining hydration.

And Moll, she won't stop dancing—not even for necessity. "You've fed already?" she yells, keeping pace with that relentless beat.

To tell the truth, I hate dancing. But it's Molly's urging that has me folding myself in with her and the Asian boy.

Moll's hand finds mine, yanks me closer. "Can we take him home with us?" she asks, hopeful in this bold change of plans.

He's not bad to look at, I suppose—if you're into that sort of thing.

My head tips a subtle nod. "Gonna have to be quiet, though; can't wake my mom."

Yeah, Molly likes boys.

And so do I, I guess.

Just in a different sort of way.

# PEEPERS CREEPERS

Erica Brynor pondered the notion of getting caught and just what she'd do with such an intrusion. The very idea of discovery at a stranger's window put her in a mind to cry—even just thinking about it. She cast herself more coward than common pervert. The girl just didn't have it in her to approach people for simple conversation like a normal person—which is the only reason she took to window-peeping in the first place.

A person can learn a lot more about someone in ten minutes of silent observation than in an hour full of bullshit conversation. At least that's how Erica saw things.

She'd grown privy to quirks and qualms believed hidden, the ones belonging to those living in her own neighborhood.

Take Mrs. Pritchett, who lives on the corner. The old gal used to be famous, a jazz singer, way back in the twenties and thirties. Ninety-something and still not ready to die just yet, she stays up late each night, a widow spinning old 78's of herself and singing along, reliving an era that'll never come back around. She knows nobody cares anymore. Nobody wants to hear stories about old New Orleans and old New York. But Erica listens. She savors every word the woman speaks inside that empty room, words meant for an audience no longer there.

During daylight hours, with the sun high and accusing, Erica rides her bike through the neighborhood, searching all those familiar faces for any intimation of her treachery. But then the night always falls, bringing along shadows deep enough to conceal a girl in her secret endeavors.

And nobody suspects a thing.

Just before midnight she swapped out her nightshirt for black jeans, black T-shirt, and a Myron Middle School ball cap—also black—which she received for winning the seventh-grade essay contest last spring. Her ritual had to remain exactly the same—even the slightest deviation could result in her immediate discovery: T-shirt goes on first, then jeans; hair—brunette—pulled into a ponytail; left shoe, then right—always tie the right shoe first. The ball cap, that was an early summer add-on, a feature made indistinguishable since most of the kids in the neighborhood own one.

She pressed an ear against her bedroom door, listened for subtleties common to a sleeping house. Her mother always watched Leno—but only his monologue. After that, well, the man just wasn't funny. Erica preferred Letterman. But she wasn't allowed to stay up that late—not even during summer vacation.

She pulled the screen from her window and climbed out into the night, eager to learn a new secret concerning any one of a dozen neighbors she knew by sight more so than by name.

Backyards offered the deepest shadows, the darkest cover.

Night lay unopened before her, waiting only for a choice to be made concerning direction and secret. She could move north, cut through the Fannerys' yard and settle in among shrubbery gathered like hooligans beneath Melody Pincer's window. Melody's a cutter—and only Erica knows about it! Being a cutter means she makes herself feel pain to relieve pain, though it's hard to believe a girl like Melody might really be suffering inside: a popular cheerleader, class valedictorian, Wellesley College in the fall.

How's that supposed to suck?

No. There'd be nothing new at Melody's window this night. A breeze carried her south toward Dunhill Street, where it crosses Maplewine. Mr. Coddington's Cape Cod staked its claim to that corner lot the way a hibernating bear would a cave. Keep away, seemed to be the general vibe from its owner. But the man, he'd never hurt anybody; he just needed time alone with the misery that had become his life—what with the divorce and all. He'd wander through the better part of a fifth most nights—usually vodka—and still manage an early rise as assistant principal of Myron Middle School. He called to mind vague memories of Erica's own long-gone father, memories that grew weak as water with each passing year.

Erica crossed Dunhill Street, met coyly the brush pile behind Billy Pike's house. This would be a tough one: to peep, or not to peep. The thing with Billy Pike, he sometimes had a girl in his room, usually doing it to her. To Erica, a situation like that was just plain gross.

She scooted through Pike property, spilled onto the Rymans' lot, took refuge behind a rose bush growing untended beneath Willa Ryman's window. Arcade Fire sang some mournful refrain through speakers turned almost too low for a proper listen.

Radio or CD? Erica wondered.

Her fingers gained grip on the brick sill; she pulled herself chin high for a first daring peep. That's the best part, the initial glimpse inside a moment not meant for spectators.

Cinnamon incense sweetened the night through the open window. A lonely candle's flame danced like Herodias's daughter in a nearby corner. Willa herself pulled long angry drags from a menthol cigarette most likely lifted from her mother's purse. Black underwear and a matching bra performed miserably at concealing bruises too fresh to be soon forgiven. Welts rose along her back in shapes of hands.

Who hit the girl? Erica wondered. And for what reason?

Willa dropped onto her bed, gave a harsh rub against a purple bruise on her leg. "Asshole," she muttered to nobody in particular.

Such a scrawny girl, all knobs and sharp angles. Boys liked her, though—the kind of boys who rode motorcycles and worked on old cars. That owed to Willa's reputation.

Maybe that's why somebody slapped her up.

*     *     *

Cory Tarver's window loomed like a bad seventies sitcom nobody ever bothered to watch—until it got canceled. After his parents kicked him out, everybody speculated on the goings-on in his basement bedroom.

Only Erica knew for certain, though.

Two words: meth lab.

*     *     *

Erica bolted across Dandelion Drive, where the streetlight had burned out almost a month ago. She stumbled between a pair of dying yew trees, fell into the cool pool of darkness surrounding the only house that far down the block.

Neighborhood kids call the man who lives there Gacy, after the famous serial killer, even though he looks nothing at all like the infamous fiend. Nobody knows his real name, what he does for a living, or even the sound of his voice.

But Erica knows.

She slipped behind a tangle of weeds burdening the ground beneath a cracked picture window facing Dandelion Drive. Forget the backyard; a soul could vanish like smoke in that overgrown mess.

The shriveled husk of an old woman slumped like a boneless entity in a worn wheelchair. Some nights she'd call the man Harold; mostly it was William, though. And he seemed partial to William, as if in this name they retained a slim thread of a past that had clearly begun to unravel.

"Ma," he called her. "Your program is on." Mid-fifties, him, maybe older; gray hair falling out; overweight by more than a few extra late-night snacks.

The woman said, "Milton Berle?"

"Uncle Milty is dead, Ma," he explained, wheeling her to a place of prominence before an ancient Magnavox lifted out of an Andy Griffith rerun. "Jay Leno is getting started."

"I don't care for that fellow," Ma complained.

"You watch him every night, Ma."

"Is that so? Well, we'll just have to see what your father has to say about that."

"Dad's dead, Ma."

"And when did this come about?"

The man fell back on a ragged recliner once blue now gone gray, popped open a Diet Coke, and rolled his eyes. "Twenty years ago, Ma. Surely you remember that much."

But then that voice came at Erica, spoken directly into her ear. "Is that you, Brynor?" His hot breath warmed her neck.

Can a heart go completely still—even just for a moment—and start itself back up again?

The night swirled around her; sweat raced a mad dash down the girl's spine. She closed her eyes and prayed it was only a hallucination, a delayed bad reaction to the HPV vaccine her mother made her take.

But the voice came again. "Are you peeping, Brynor?" His hand found the small of her back; he followed her closer to the ground in a squat. "I thought I was the only one peeping in this neighborhood."

Erica dared a glance, to put a face with the voice:

Billy Pike, the one who does it to his girlfriend.

A lie found its way into her mouth. "I wasn't peeping."

"Sure looked like it to me." He gained his feet, had a quick peek inside the window, returned to her with all his accusations intact. "You do this every night?"

In the pale light leaking from the window, Erica studied the boy's features. "A couple times a week," she admitted.

"Erica Brynor, nasty girl of the night," he teased. "I always knew there was something else beneath that quiet-girl routine."

"And what's your excuse?"

A grin bent his lips. "I just like to watch."

*   *   *

They followed a path cutting through a woods behind Pequot Elementary, into a neighborhood unfamiliar to Erica. Billy pointed toward this house and that, giving up names, dishing dirt on deeds done behind closed doors.

"There's an awful lot of strange goings-on in these parts," he explained, spreading his arms wide. "Take the Lipnickies here." His head bent toward a house on the corner. "Young married couple, so lovey-dovey in the daytime, but come night they sleep in separate rooms. And it's not like they argue, either."

He was nice to look at, this Billy Pike. Beneath the streetlight his eyes took on a soft brown glow.

"Come on," he said, taking her hand, pulling her along as he traipsed into the backyard of a newer brick ranch house. "This is Miss Turnbull's place. She teaches kindergarten at Pequot."

Erica's hands grasped the sill; she flung a lazy gaze through the open window. "Oh my gosh!" she hollered.

The woman spun around, fixed her eyes on the young interloper, and gasped. "How dare you intrude!" She bolted toward the door and swore swift punishment, should she lay hold on the girl.

Billy ran left; Erica scampered right, zooming past her irate pursuer, barely escaping an outstretched arm.

"Can you believe that shit?" the boy said, sucking down great gulps of air at the top of the street. "And she's a kindergarten teacher!"

Erica struggled to catch her breath between fits of nervous giggles. "She'd have killed me," she said, "had she caught me."

"Uh-uh. She'd have done to you what she was doing to him."

"Eww! Don't say that!" She tested boundaries of this new-found ally and spilled a confession. "I peeped you before, a couple of times. You were in your room with a girl."

Billy Pike ran silent for a moment, like maybe he needed to mull over the possibilities of all she might have seen. Or maybe she'd crossed one of those boundaries an ally ought never cross—or at least not mention once the breach occurs. But if Billy took offense, he never let on. "Ex-girlfriend," he said, eyeing the girl in the soft glow of a low summer moon. "And I've peeped you—a time or three."

It was Erica's turn to mull those possibilities, to ponder compromising positions she may or may not have engaged in recently. "I'm okay with that," she finally admitted.

Billy's head tipped a nod so subtle but clear in its intent.

What they saw, well—they'd allow each other those secrets.

At least for now.

They left off in front of the Brynor house with the gray of dawn etching the beginnings of another day along the edges of an expiring night.

His hand found hers. "You, ah, wanna do this again maybe?"

"You mean peep?"

"Why not? We make a great team."

"Sure," she said, breaking loose of him. "But next time, let's skip the kindergarten teachers."

# Bodies Terrestrial

Jimmy McNamara's hand lingered atop that skinny shifter, eagerly awaiting the jump from second to third gear and the growing speed meant to fling the shiny borrowed Ford Model T beyond Caulfield city limits, out to where that *rat-a-tat-tat* wouldn't draw much commotion from folks who'd know its meaning.

Teagan Barton had other notions, though.

"There it is again!" he hollered from the passenger seat. "Right over Draper's place." The boy's fingers gripped that long black case taking its leisure on his lap; his eyes fixed on some point in the clear blue above.

Jimmy couldn't see it, though. "You sure it ain't only a bird?"

Righteous indignation like a shaken-up bottle of soda pop bubbled over the boy. "It's a goddamn airplane, man! A red biplane!" He jerked his gaze a-loose of the sky and flung it at his friend behind the wheel. "You ever seen a bird with two sets of wings? 'Cause I ain't."

Jimmy's head tipped subtlely, his eyes took up a search of their own. "Must be like you said, then."

"I ain't seen many," admitted Teagan, "but I know a plane when I see one."

"Maybe we oughtn't go shooting that thing, huh?" Jimmy said.

Teagan's hands tapped some vague rhythm against that black case. "Ain't no airplane flyer gonna know what we're doing. Besides, up there he can see clear down to Biloxi—maybe even to the Gulf. He ain't watching us."

Jimmy set the Model T onto Calfton Road, put them to a crawl while scanning overhead for spies.

Teagan's the one who saw her first, that tiny speck of a girl wandering along the middle of the road, head tipped back, eyes searching the sky.

"Ain't that Grace Ann Folmer?" he asked.

Jimmy gave a nod, goosed the gas to gain some speed.

Teagan said, "Talk her into going with us."

"What for?"

"'Cause she's nice to look at."

"She's only a kid—not even old enough to know better."

Teagan argued, "Just a couple years younger than us. That ain't a lot."

Jimmy said, "You the one gonna ask her daddy can she go?"

He wouldn't. Charles Folmer was a man big enough to whip Jack Dempsey himself—just for fun.

Jimmy brought the Ford still; his finger punched the klaxon's button. *Ahh-ooh-gahh!*

The girl jumped on the driver's running board, cast her blue-eyed gaze around the car's interior, asked, "Who'd ya swipe this from?"

"Didn't swipe it," Jimmy tut-tutted.

"I'm gonna get me one just like it," Grace Ann promised.

Hair the color of honey in a clear glass jar, this girl. Lips pink and swollen, like maybe a bee stuck her one good. It was a natural thing on Grace Ann, though, lips like hers.

Teagan's eyes settled on her mouth. "Girls can't drive no Model T," he told her.

She leaned through the window like she meant to get a hold on the boy, said, "It's nineteen twenty-two. Girls can do anything a stupid old boy can do. They even got women airplane flyers now."

Teagan got bold with the matter, said, "Girl can't piss on a wall."

Grace Ann wouldn't be dissuaded. "Betcha I can."

"I'd pay to see that!"

"How much?"

Jimmy's hand found the top of her head, gently eased the girl back through the window. "Ain't nobody gonna pay to watch you make water," he said.

But Grace Ann had moved on. "What's in the case?"

"Tommy gun," Jimmy confessed.

"Nuh-uh," the girl argued. "You ain't got no tommy gun."

Teagan Barton popped the locks, flipped the lid, showed off that black metal and dark wood, and told all about their plans to go squirrel hunting.

"Won't be no meat left, you shoot it with that," Grace observed.

Jimmy's laughter settled the matter. "We're only gonna shoot at some trees maybe."

Typical for Grace, a whine crawled between the girl's words. "I wanna shoot it too."

Teagan said, "I'll let you shoot it."

But Jimmy's the one always thought things through. "And what of her daddy?"

"Daddy don't have to know," Grace assured all who'd listen. "Besides, he thinks I'm off traipsing with Selma Downey, won't be expecting me till supper."

Jimmy opened his door, said, "He whips my ass, I'm whipping yours, girl."

"Fair enough."

Jimmy would never lift a hand to her, though. Grace Ann Folmer pretty much did whatever she wanted—same as her mama before her. Some girls can just get away with stuff.

She took up perch in the middle, straight between those boys. Though she had always favored Jimmy, her body leaned closest to Teagan.

"Did y'all see the plane?" she asked.

Teagan breathed in, drew on her scent. It had nothing to do with perfume or soap; it was a natural thing, something sweet, girlish. The sort of scent that would stick in a boy's head, have him conjuring recollections of Grace long after she'd moved on to fancy boys from higher stations than Mississippi could ever manage.

Her hand found that black case, gave it a knowing pat. "Where'd ya get it?"

Teagan said, "It's my pop's."

"He rob banks?"

"Runs hooch."

"Won't he miss it?"

Teagan grinned. "He's in jail at the moment."

Jimmy wrestled the car onto the lane cutting right through Tockett's Wood, out to where old Mavis Tockett once had a house. Nobody came back there much anymore. Wasn't anything to see but trees and what remained of a cabin.

Teagan's eyes, they were busy with Grace Ann, memorizing her dainty hands with their chewed up nails, those delicate fine hairs on tanned arms, and scuffed knees showing off beneath the hem of her gray dress.

Teagan said, "Heard you socked Richie Tockett in his eye."

"Yup!" said the girl. "Got it all nice and swolled shut, too."

Jimmy set the Ford to a stop near to where the foundation of a vanished barn could still be deciphered among tall grass. "Why'd ya hit him?" he asked.

Grace Ann offered little. "Got my reasons."

Doors opened, bodies spilled from the car. Teagan's the one those other two flocked around.

Having a Thompson will do that.

"I'll go first," he announced, uncasing the beast. The boy affixed that round clip, aimed it at a low mound of dirt piled right beside the remains of a roofless cabin, and let loose a *rat-a-tat-tat!* folks a mile away could surely hear.

Twenty or thirty rounds tore up the earth in that one spot, sent dust and dirt into the air like the mess of a devil.

When the moment cleared and the calm commenced all over again, ears went to ringing while birds held their tongues.

"Lord Almighty!" the girl exclaimed.

"You're next," Teagan assured her, drawing her closer to his side.

She got hold on the gun, tested its heft, proclaimed it "Awful heavy," and true to a know-it-all girl, she pulled down on the trigger before the boy had time to issue whatnots and wherefores.

The black barrel kicked high, threw lead at the sky, knocked the tiny girl ass-over-shoulders into the grass, left her dress belly high, her legs splayed, and put those clean white underpants on show for all to see.

And Grace Ann didn't cry, neither, the way Teagan's kid brother cried when he, too, took that same sort of spill. Grace, she just sat up, righted her dress, worked an easy rub against her shoulder, and pronounced, "Awful mean kick, that."

She threw in a stray "Jeez Louise" and a mumbled thing sounded like "Lord Almighty" before she gained her feet, swept grass from her clothing, and took up that Thompson for another go.

Didn't take no college boy to recognize an opportunity presented. Teagan Barton got behind the girl, pressed his body against hers, his front to her back.

"Gotta do this right," he said, that right hand of his finding rest right beneath her belly button. His lips brushed her ear; words came soft as the girl's own skin. "I'm gonna hold you up, all right?"

Grace said, "Okay, then."

Instruction concerning keeping the gun's butt tucked tight to her shoulder followed. "*Squeeze* the trigger," the boy counseled, "don't just pull."

A sudden burst tore further into that dirt mound, exposed things that didn't quite resemble stick nor stone.

Jimmy saw it first, asked, "Are those bones?"

Teagan snatched the gun, returned it to its case, and followed Jimmy over to the mound.

Grace Ann, she's the one spelled things out, put it in plain old English.

"That right there," she announced, "was once a person."

*   *   *

"Mavis Tockett," said Sheriff Gomes. "Died of the influenza back near four years ago."

Grace Ann's the one took up that children's rhyme. "Had a little bird, his name was Enza, I opened the window and in flew Enza."

Jimmy said, "You remember that?"

Her head tipped a subtle nod. "I was in second grade when it came here," she said, sharing recollections of when all that dying swept through the world during 1918. "Lost my granddaddy on my mama's side on account of it."

Sheriff's chin dropped, taking his gaze to the ground. "We all lost somebody in that mess," he said.

Mouths went quiet while the four watched a pair of men from Mr. Glickman's funeral parlor remove Mavis Tockett's remains from that shallow hole.

"Bodies terrestrial," Jimmy proclaimed, "—like in First Corinthians."

Grace Ann asked, "What's it mean?"

"Means we all go back to dust—same as Mavis."

Even the pretty ones, Teagan thought, eyeing the dainty girl at his side. "How come they're wearing masks over their mouths?" he asked, sliding his gaze toward those funeral fellas.

That's when Sheriff Gomes tied a mask around his own head and broke the news nobody wanted to hear. "Gonna have to quarantine y'all over to Jackson."

*   *   *

Doctors separated the three for a time, just long enough to pace them through extra hot showers, draw blood, ask questions concerning how they came to dig up old Mavis, possibly disturbing more than just a pile of bones.

Jimmy and Teagan were first inside the room they'd share until whatever needed doing got done. The simple space harbored three fugitive cots, a card table, three folding chairs, and a game of checkers meant to occupy the attentions of no more than two at a time.

"Coulda brung us one of them new radio things," Teagan complained, dropping onto one of those cots. "And where's Grace Ann, anyway?"

Jimmy took up with a folding chair, turned talk toward words he'd heard from folks in charge, how it didn't seem likely a pile of bones might still carry disease enough to trouble the living. "Forty-eight hours, is all they want from us."

Teagan issued displeasure. "We gotta stay for two days?"

That's when all the hollering began, somewhere in that hallway outside their room, Grace Ann's voice rising above those belonging to nurses.

"You ain't the boss of me!" the girl bellowed.

Some fool nurse took up the challenge, said, "Don't you sass me, missy!"

Grace Ann gave it right back. "Then come over here and get you some!"

"Git!" barked a nurse. "Git on in there, you awful heathen child."

"Chicken liver!" The girl barged into the room, slammed the door in her wake, announced, "They ain't sticking me back there just to test my temperature." She rolled up on Jimmy, snatched the boy's hand and put it against her forehead. "Do I feel hot?"

She sported a pea-green gown similar to the ones issued to the boys. But Grace's gown had come a-loose around back, offering Teagan a lingering gawk at the stark whiteness of the girl's exposed bottom.

"You gotta quit fussing with folks, Grace Ann," Jimmy said. "I mean, if you ain't socking some fool boy, you're having words with 'em."

She took umbrage with his remarks, went nose to nose with her accuser. "Even my own mama don't take my temperature that way any-more."

"And what of Richie Tockett?" the boy argued. "He can't see spit out of that eye you closed for him."

Grace Ann's spine hitched up real straight. "He had it coming," is what she said.

Inside Teagan's head, notions went to flirting with the boy, nudging him toward laying a pinch to one of those lily white cheeks, or maybe even a playful swat—just to coerce the girl's attentions to himself.

But Jimmy McNamara, he'd not allow such displays of familiarity. He traipsed after Teagan's bold gaze, found it fixed to the girl's exposure, spun Grace ass-backward to him, and tied up her gown—just the way Teagan knew he would.

"Spoil sport," said Teagan, tossing onto his side, giving those other two his back.

*    *    *

A silvery spill of moonlight splashed against the girl, gave away her escape from her own cot, caught her bold march toward Jimmy's place of rest. And that boy wouldn't deny her, neither. He just yanked back his sheet, and let the girl climb in beside him.

Teagan Barton feigned sleep, watching the two through midnight shad-ows gathered in the darkened room. Jimmy wouldn't fool with her, though. Even Teagan knew that much. Jimmy preferred older girls, with big boobs and curvy hips. Grace Ann, well, she was flat as a board and just as straight. A kid, is all.

"You ever been kissed?" Jimmy's question came wrapped in a whisper not meant to reach Teagan's cot.

But it did.

Grace Ann said, "Course I have."

Jimmy's laugh came soft, giddy-like. "Ain't talking about kissing your mama and daddy."

"Oh. You mean kiss a boy."

Jimmy's the one who instigated it, dipped his head, pressed his lips to hers, a quick thing really, not unlike a friendly peck—at least that's how Teagan explained it to himself.

It might have been anger, that twist he felt in his gut. Probably just jealousy, though. Didn't seem fair, this scene. Teagan's the one who liked the girl.

Jimmy's voice fell soft against the night. "Why'd you sock Richie Tockett?"

Grace Ann said, "Kiss me again and I just might tell you."

Jimmy—bless his soul—blurted, "Teagan has a crush on you."

The girl raised her head from their shared pillow, tossed her gaze toward the boy feigning sleep. "He said my mama serves the devil," she announced. "Said she's a witch—on account of she reads palms and such."

Jimmy sat up, fixed his eyes to the one minding his own business. "Teagan said that?"

"Uh-uh. Richie Tockett said so," Grace clarified. "That's how come I socked him in his eye."

Jimmy fell back against his pillow, let quiet settle back in among them. He whispered a thing sounded like, "He don't know your mama," and drifted away from the rest of them.

Grace Ann flung her feet to the floor and traipsed back to her own cot.

*   *   *

Grace Ann worked at her third bowl of ice cream—strawberry. She pulled a triple jump across the checker board, said, "Crown me" to Jimmy McNamara, all the while keeping her blue-eyed gawk fixed tightly to Teagan lying on his cot.

The boy stared back, held her gaze the way he'd gladly hold her hand—

if she had a mind for such a gesture.

"Wanna play?" she asked, her question aimed at Teagan.

Jimmy protested the invite. "We ain't even done yet, Grace Ann."

But the girl cut another quick move, dropped a double jump on the whining boy, lifted his last two pieces from the board, and announced, "That's game."

Teagan settled into Jimmy's vacated seat, tipped a nod toward that now-empty ice cream bowl, and said, "Gonna go right through you, you keep eating that stuff."

"They ain't gonna let us take any to home," she explained, "so we best get it while we can."

Checkers filled the board, jumping commenced here and there, each side laying claim to the other's captured pieces.

Grace Ann won the first game straightaway. Took the second one as well—though just barely. Teagan had her trapped in the third, where any old move would end in certain defeat.

The girl's dainty fingers reached for a piece but pulled back.

Teagan asked, "What'll you give me if I win this game?" He leaned back in his chair, let a grin bend his lips. "Will ya let me kiss you?"

She went for that same checker again, lifted it from its square, said, "You ain't gonna win," and fell into a triple jump the boy never contemplated. "Crown me, Teagan Barton."

Before Teagan could even consider the girl's sudden escape, their room door yawned wide and coughed up the sturdy figure of Sheriff Gomes.

The lawman wandered through the scene like he meant to investigate the goings-on of the morning, made pronouncements on all he saw. "Ice cream and checkers, huh?" he said, hands on hips. "Well I guess being young is the life."

Grace Ann's the one who spoke up. "Ain't you scared of catching the influenza?—you not wearing a mask and all."

Something akin to a smirk curled around the man's mouth. "Ain't in any danger," he announced. "And neither are you lot. Seems them bones don't belong to Mavis Tockett after all—at least to hear her kin tell of it. They claim she's buried over to Carsonville, right beside her folks."

Jimmy took hold of the question most needing asking. "Then who are them bones we found?"

"Could be anybody, I reckon," said Sheriff. "Probably been there for a coon's age."

"Bodies terrestrial," Jimmy proclaimed, sounding wise as any preacher ever did.

"Back to dust," chimed Grace Ann.

Teagan's hand brushed hers. "Even the pretty ones." He said it aloud this time, said it twice. "Even the pretty ones."

Grace Ann slipped her hand inside his, gave the boy a smile. She understood him just fine.

# Bigfoot Was My Father

The word had spread like locusts in Moses's neighborhood. It even made the local news. A few seemingly normal individuals made claims of having actually glimpsed the mythical, the strange, the other-worldly. A farmer stood before television cameras telling the community that he'd seen it with his own two eyes, wandering a worn path near his cornfield. A school teacher followed a week later, assuring all who'd listen that she, too, had a run-in with this forgotten relic of evolution. Others came forward as well; respectable people, each and every one, claiming their own encounter with the beast of many names. Sasquatch. Yeti. The Abominable Snowman. But back in the summer of 1977, we all took to calling the legend Bigfoot.

Some witnesses even carried plaster castings to their all-important news conferences. These plaster castings of massive footprints put a fear in those of us who were young enough to believe such a creature could—and probably did—exist in the woods near our homes. And there was little doubt these beasts had a taste for human flesh and blood.

A walk through the back forty now promised carnage to those too slow to outrun an almost-certain encounter. Dares were issued. Goosebumps mingled with adrenaline as the brave ones took up the challenge.

Finally, the day came; I saw the beastly devil with my own two eyes. It hid among the tall grass, crouching low to the ground, doing its absolute best to go undetected, expecting a quick and easy snack.

What I actually saw, though, turned out to be nothing more than a tree stump. But in my ten-year-old mind, that tree stump had long hairy arms and legs, black soulless eyes filled with hunger and hatred, and a notion for tasting blood.

*My* blood!

I bolted toward the house, every so often tossing glances over my shoulder, certain I'd see the tell-tale loping gait of a monster in fast pursuit.

I saw nothing, though—nothing but trees and weeds and clear blue sky.

Breathless and filled with the rush of having just cheated death, I told my tale of facing the Devil himself to my sister, my brothers, and to a few friends. Eventually the story made its way to my father's ears.

"No such thing, son," Dad assured me, certain in his pronouncement.

We wandered back to the scene of my epic showdown with the hairy vision from hell, discovering in its place the afore-mentioned tree stump. The lack of footprints or any other form of irrefutable evidence gave weight to my father's assumption that Bigfoot does not exist—at least not in *our* woods.

Then it showed itself, that sparkle of mischief in Dad's eyes.

"Come on," he said. "Let's have a little fun with this."

We wandered back to the house, excited at the possibilities of what Dad had in mind.

A quick search of the closet produced a fur coat; a brown, long-haired thing that ran the length of a person's body.

Dad slipped into the coat, hunched beneath it, his head hidden. "This will work," he announced.

Work for *what?* we kids all wondered.

Dad grabbed his Polaroid camera and the fur coat, and made for the back forty again with us kids in tow.

Just around the bend, near where I swore I'd seen the real monster, my dad donned the coat, drifted into the tall grass and brush, and crouched low to the ground. Two pictures were produced that day; pictures illustrating a large brown hairy thing hiding in the grass.

"Oh my *gosh!*" my sister's friend Susan exclaimed upon viewing the evidence. "I am *never* going out there again."

We let her believe the lie for a day or two—if I remember correctly.

Others saw the pictures, too, and were given varying versions of how Bigfoot happened to be captured on film.

We always revealed the truth of the matter; we never left a soul to believe the hoax. It was *Candid Camera* or *MTV's Punk'd* on a smaller scale. To us kids, it smacked of pure genius!

The story faded over the years, recalled from time to time with a laugh, a shake of the head, and a fond smile.

My father passed away in May 2012 after suffering a massive heart attack. Since his passing, I find myself pondering those long-forgotten memories with greater frequency. I guess there's some truth to the idea that a person never truly dies as long as there's somebody around to remember the little things.

Thanks for the memories, Dad.

# BEAUTIFUL CHAOS

Darcy Minzer didn't care much for labels; she just considered herself open-minded, into the moment—whatever *that* may bring. Like last night, at the club. Females aren't necessarily her preference, mind you, but this one here, the girl lying asleep beside her, she told a good story, made an interesting promise or three, maybe even twisted the truth just a little. Didn't matter; talked her way in, she did.

Scrutiny had a go at her promises.

And that twisted truth, it sort of fell to the floor in wicked knots.

The girl made good on the meat of it, though, that thing Darcy craved most. Without this one here, Darcy might not have known, might never have even suspected.

The girl—Wendy, isn't it?—lay against the mattress, sprawled face down, dainty hands tucked beneath a pillow, the rhythm of her breathing keeping time.

Such a small thing, really; young enough to be Darcy's daughter—if Darcy had been inclined to have had a daughter. Her bare body, stark in its whiteness, hinted a mix of sex and vanilla extract. A curious scent, that. And natural, too, if the girl could be believed.

Strawberry blond spilled down her back in a tangled mess reminiscent of that actress girl, the one always at odds with the law.

Nice to look at, though.

And eager, too.

Darcy's feet hit the floor with a soft thud. She snatched up her bathrobe and drifted toward the living room for another look—just to be sure.

She'd watched it the night before, just once, that grainy image on her computer screen. Still, she couldn't ratify the face laying claim to that name—*his* name—even after twenty-odd years. Yeah, she'd admit a resemblance—though only slightly in degree. And sure, people change—especially after two decades.

But still…

She played the video again and again, set about deciphering movements and mannerisms meant to betray this obvious imposter. But those movements and mannerisms, they belonged to *him*.

So did that voice.

He sang the song just the way he did on the album.

Darcy's weight shifted against the hard plastic chair; her fingers worked at the keyboard, brought up that image for another view.

The one calling himself Avis Atwater trod a dark stage in a dive somewhere outside of Denver, a familiar black guitar slung low, favoring his right hip. Custom built, that guitar, back in eighty-eight, made special for his twenty-first birthday.

A gift from Darcy.

But even a fact like that didn't prove anything. Pictures of Avis and the instrument had graced more than a few magazine covers in the years since the accident. A good eye and the right tools could easily replicate the thing—should someone be so inclined.

Faces backing this version of Avis—a drummer and bass player—retained boyish intensity too recent to recollect any goings-on way back when. They might not have even drawn breath before 1988, before that moment responsible for ending something so promising. Easy marks, they'd be; fools for an image that came undone long before ever fully forming.

Darcy's cell phone chirped, yanked the woman back through the years, flung her down in a reality of which she'd long ago grown weary.

"I'd need to see more to be certain," claimed a familiar voice, "but I'm leaning toward it being him."

It couldn't be, though, and Darcy said as much. "You saw him same as I did, Ricky. Persistently vegetative, that doctor promised."

Silence as thick as margarine buttered the moment before Ricky Kulkrick fully committed. "You asked my opinion last night. If that's not Avis, then his ghost is out there playing his songs."

"A vegetable," is what Darcy said. "People don't come back from a thing like brain damage."

"Avis could—you of all people know his stubborn streak."

Darcy's sigh came swollen, a thing ripe with frustration. "Suppose we go and see him?"

"See who?"

"Avis," she said.

"If he'd wanted anything to do with us—"

"At the nursing home," Darcy explained. "We can put this mess to rest."

Ricky had other thoughts, though. "You don't need *me* for that. Go and see for yourself."

＊　　＊　　＊

"So, um, am I staying over again?" Wendy trickled in like a slow leak, pooled beside the desk, and shifted on her feet like a naughty schoolgirl in the principal's office. A white Arcade Fire T-shirt highlighted the shapes of her breasts; tight jeans hugged the rest of her contours. "I mean, because you promised…"

They'd talked about it last night, briefly, during their post-coital chit-chat. But the tone had been decidedly noncommittal—at least on Darcy's part.

"How about I call you?" Darcy proposed.

Wendy swiped a pad of Post-It notes from the desk, scribbled her dig-its, and stuck the guilty note to the computer screen.

Darcy eyed the yellow scrap of paper like she meant to commit the numbers to memory. "What's your last name?" she asked.

"Limus."

"How'd you come across the video?"

The girl flinched a nervous shrug, told a story concerning an uncle, how he'd been in Denver a few months back, saw Avis at a club, sent her the image over the phone. "I posted it on YouTube right away."

Darcy needed to know. "Why tell *me* about it?"

There went that flinch again. "Just figured you'd want to know."

*    *    *

They'd once shared all things common, Avis and Darcy; high school sweethearts, they'd been, long before he allowed her to breach the inner sanctum and bang drums in his band. But even that, the drumming part, had only been an angle, a move meant to help distinguish Beautiful Chaos from every other rock group scratching for attention on the local club scene. Female drummers will get a band noticed—especially the cute ones.

To recall Avis telling it, Darcy Minzer wore cuteness like a comfortable T-shirt.; brunette hair down to her shoulders, green eyes like a china doll's. A petite package, that girl, with just enough curves in all the places any straight boy hoped to find them.

Darcy bore a bold streak, too, playing drums in skimpy little get-ups. Show enough skin and you were assured of steady-paying gigs among those frat houses on campus.

Twenty-five years can issue awful updates on a human body, though; brunette turns gray; curves go doughy; girlish charm dries up worse than two-day old toast.

She could still play those drums, though; plays better than most guys. But a thing like talent, it can put a girl at odds with the ruling elite. Can't go running circles around boys, laying shame to their game.

Suppose it *is* Avis in that video?—though Darcy clung tightly to doubt. Why didn't he contact her and Ricky? Certainly a Beautiful Chaos reunion offered greater potential than just Avis alone might manage.

They'd been special once—if only for a moment. Darcy still had the album to prove it. They'd caught a groove that summer, fell into a deep pocket, put down those ten songs Avis wrote and polished to a high shine. Three parts working together as one.

Thing is, it didn't last.

And talent—or lack of—had nothing to do with it.

*     *     *

"The big forty-five, huh?" Donnie Corver's arms went easily around Darcy's meager shape. He administered that familiar hug, the sort of hug possessing bone-breaking potential. But Donnie, he'd never hurt a soul. "Well happy birthday, girlie. And welcome to old age."

Darcy pulled free from the giant, wandered deeper inside his lair, and took rest on a sagging leather sofa that no doubt came into its first moments during the Seventies. Everything in that cluttered space, in fact, reeked of some other decade—besides the one currently in charge.

"You ever going to update," she asked, "you know, get modern?"

Donnie settled beside her, let his hands rest on his knees. "Ain't got no use for all that fancy stuff," he explained.

Darcy's gaze rolled across the floor like a favorite old marble. "A vacuum cleaner isn't considered fancy anymore," she assured the man.

"A broom works just as well." His bulk shifted, rattled that old sofa. "But you ain't here to discuss my housekeeping, are you?"

Donnie gigged with Chaos way back when; equipment setup, mostly. But his size, *that's* what assured club owners the band would be paid the full amount agreed upon.

Darcy smoothed a wrinkle from that faded Led Zeppelin T-shirt clinging tightly to her shape. She sifted a pile of words in her mind before deciding on direction. "When's the last time you visited Avis?"

Donnie's meaty hand rubbed at that stubble on his chin; he pondered the question floating in the space between them. "Been an awful long time,

I suppose. Ten years, I guess. But I ain't the only one who stopped going up to see the man."

Darcy said, "I'm not looking to blame anybody for anything." She gained her feet, jammed her hands in the pockets of her jeans, and laid down a slow pace meant to draw the moment into its proper context. "I don't think anybody has been to see him in a long stretch."

"Well shoot," Donnie protested. "Ricky's his best friend. And *he* ain't been to see him since right after… I mean, at least *some* of us kept going for a spell."

"Why'd you stop?"

"Because he ain't there. He don't know anybody anymore. Even those doctors said Avis ain't aware of nothing going on around him."

Darcy's pace went still. "Do you think he could recover?"

Donnie's head wagged left and right. "Not a chance," he said. "His brain's been scrambled, girlie. You heard those doctors."

"Could be they were wrong."

Donnie scoffed. "When's the last time *you* were up there to see him?"

Sharp needles of shame etched guilty tattoos all across her skin, painted the girl as no better than the others. She'd abandoned Avis just as surely as those others had.

"He's on YouTube," she said. "A video of some club gig in Denver."

"Bullshit."

"Ricky thinks it's him."

"Maybe Ricky's back to banging dope."

"And *I'm* thinking it's him. Maybe."

Donnie's head tossed up that wag again. "Ain't no way he's up and about." His mass came loose from the sofa, angled toward the picture window overlooking Portland Street out front. "That part of the story is over."

The truth of his words sported spines of the prickly sort, sharp enough to draw blood and bad intentions, opening wounds that never really closed.

Darcy dropped onto the sofa again and thought to change direction.

"Are you still messing with that April woman?"

Donnie snorted his derision at the mention of that name, said, "I ain't seen her in nearly two years." He drifted closer, propped his weight against the sofa's arm. "How about you? You going guy or girl these days?"

"Neither," she said, "—till last night." Darcy fell into a rhythmic explanation concerning Wendy Limus and the goings-on of the previous twenty-four hours; told how the girl pulled up that video, brought back the past in full grainy color.

Donnie asked, "Who's her uncle?"

"Don't know," Darcy said. "Claims he shot the video, though."

"Denver, huh?"

"So she says."

"Gonna go see him?"

Darcy pondered the question, answered with one of her own. "See who? Avis or the uncle?"

Donnie shrugged. "Don't matter which, I suppose."

"I've got to do *something*," said Darcy, taking to her feet again. "The mystery's already been built up."

*     *     *

*"Avis Atwater?"* The receptionist peered over the top of her glasses, acted as if Darcy might not have all her screws tightened. "What do you want with Avis Atwater? Are you *family*?"

Not exactly family, Darcy tried to explain. "But I once was engaged to him—before the accident, of course. I played drums in his band—"

"I *know* who you are." Like poison from her tongue those words fell onto the reception desk. "That whole bunch of you, his best *friends*—when it looked like he'd be rich and famous!" The woman nudged her glasses higher up the bridge of her thin nose. "But where were any of you people while he sat up in here year after year, rarely getting visits?"

There'd been a million and one excuses, those flimsy reasons why

Darcy couldn't make it in to see the boy she'd once meant to marry:

The antiseptic smell of the nursing home turned her stomach.

All of those souls just waiting for death to claim them simply depressed her too much.

Avis, he wouldn't even know who's there and who isn't.

"Avis isn't here anymore," the woman claimed, leaning across the desk. "He left Birch Run Manor five years ago."

*Left?*

And just how did he *leave?* Darcy wondered, unable to bring sound to those words.

"Maybe he just got better and walked himself right out that front door one fine day." Sarcasm dripped from the woman's words. "Or maybe it was a cousin who claimed him, gave him a home and friendship."

Darcy found her strength again, spoke against this lie. "He didn't have any cousins."

"Did so."

"He never met his father and his mother died three years after the accident. No siblings, no surviving relatives—"

"The son of his father's sister," the reception lady argued. "He had all his paperwork in order. We don't just turn patients loose—even if they *can't* afford to stay." Her back went straight, as if somebody sneaked up behind her and rammed a stick up her ass. "Besides, that cousin is the only one who came to visit Avis faithfully across all those years."

*    *    *

"He's playing in a club up in Piedmont," Darcy explained, certain Ricky Kulkrick wouldn't waste time chasing a phantom.

But the Indian surprised her. "If you're in the mood to drive, I'll ride up there with you."

*    *    *

The Zoo occupied its usual place along the 615 Corridor just outside Piedmont city limits—right where it had been twenty-odd years earlier, back when Beautiful Chaos last played the club.

Darcy angled her Toyota into the lot, squeezed the car between a pair faded yellow stripes, killed the engine, and listened to the low rumble of music seeping through the building's walls.

Ricky's the one who spoke the song's title aloud. "'Breakdown,'" he said. "I can tell by the beat."

Darcy knew it too. She's the one who came up with that nasty beat; laid it atop a song Avis intended to record with only guitar and vocal. That's how she earned her only writing credit.

She shifted in her seat, set her gaze upon Ricky? "You ready to figure this thing out?"

*    *    *

He moved across that stage with a familiar cat-like strut, wearing that low-slung black guitar on his hip. Those long fingers walked between the frets like they'd always been there; as if twenty-odd years hadn't occurred. And from the view by the front door, he could easily pass for Avis.

But up close, though, that's where the charade failed.

Oh, sure, those who didn't know the man might not decipher the difference.

Darcy cracked that code, though. She knew the boy before the man.

"Even after the accident," Ricky said, "Avis still looked like Avis. This guy, he's not him."

A stray thought drifted through Darcy's head. "He could pass," she said, though barely loud enough to top the pounding music. "In a pinch, I mean."

"Pass for what?" Ricky's gaze bounced between Darcy and the imposter.

It was only a thought—a brief one at that. But Darcy spoke it aloud.

"A reunion. Everybody here believes he's Avis."

It could never happen, though. There were just too many people who'd be able to blow the charade. Nobody would want *that* on their resume.

"I'll talk to my lawyer," Ricky conceded, "have him draw up a cease and desist."

It couldn't go *that* way either.

"Leave him be," Darcy said, moving for the exit. "We missed him while he was here. Let these people enjoy him now that he's gone."

# FRIDAY NIGHT AGAIN

Friday night again.

Fridays always got there too fast.

The shuffling outside of her bedroom door told on him, ratted him out the way *she'd* never be brave enough to do. He'd be in there soon enough. Too soon, you ask her.

Lying in bed, Jamie tossed onto her back, pulled up an image from summer past, to the time when she'd stayed out to Grandma Sweeney's farm, way out in the country, away from Stanley and his stupid drunken self. At least at Grandma's there weren't any boys or men to say what's what about how things were going to be—like it or not. Green fields filled with alfalfa—those were the best recollections. All that country air scented with tilled earth and fresh-cut grass!

Couldn't get *that* here in the city. All the city offers is dirt and stink—and stupid old Stanley.

The bang of his work boots put the man just outside her door. He'd wait a moment, testing the air, seeing if he might get away with it just one more time.

She told Mother Jen once, back when it first started.

"Just be glad you have a roof over your head, Miss Priss," is all Mother Jen had to say on the subject.

The loose doorknob gave up a familiar jiggle; the door yawned just wide enough for Stanley to peer inside the room. Greasy yellow light leaked into the moment from somewhere outside—that old streetlamp out front, maybe.

His boots came off in the hallway.

Mother Jen's specter stepped into that puddle of light, her lips met

Stanley's ear. "Leave her be tonight, Stan," she whispered into his head.

Stanley's protest stank of lies. "I ain't never put no hand to that little bitch, Jen. God's truth."

But Mother Jen, she knew better—though she'd never lift a finger to put a halt to the goings-on beneath her own roof. She needed Stanley the same way she needed that extra money the State of Wisconsin paid her to look after foster kids like Jamie.

"Well I won't compete," Mother Jen swore, "—not with no kid, I won't."

"Ain't nobody saying you have to." Stanley followed her back toward the living room, dropping low-intentioned words along the way. Even with his departure the room still reeked of whiskey and his sweat.

He'd be back, though, just as soon as Mother Jen left for her midnight shift at the Gas & Go.

In her mind's eye, in that safe place she'd constructed since the accident took her mother and little brother, Jamie would get to stay with Grandma Sweeney all the time—and Stanley would go to jail forever.

But that couldn't ever happen—not as long as Mother Jen kept custody.

*    *    *

It's the wood smoke that woke Jamie from that brief piece of sleep she hoped would carry her through to the morning, unaware of whether Stanley had bothered with her or not. Wood smoke, not the usual smell of the oil-burning space heater Mother Jen kept in the living room during the cold winter months.

Jamie's bare feet found the chilled sting of the floorboards. She dared a peek past that worthless bedroom door that did next to nothing to keep her safe—until tonight.

Through the smoky haze her eyes found that lazy shape passed out on the sofa.

Angry flames licked paint from the walls around him.

Stanley would die there without Jamie waking him from his stupor.

But Jamie's own legs wouldn't allow her to save the man. They simply carried her to the window, sent a message to her arms, convinced them to push open the glass, thus granting arms, legs, and the attached girl, a means to escape.

*　　*　　*

The fire department determined the blaze started when that oil-burning space heater ignited the curtains, delivering Stanley and the entire house to the flames of hell.

Mother Jen, well, she found solace in knowing Stanley probably hadn't suffered much. All that whiskey, the medical examiner claimed, had pretty much rendered the man comatose before the fire had engulfed the house.

Even so, Jamie's dream never did come to pass. The State of Wisconsin deemed Grandma Sweeney too old to care for a young girl of Jamie's age. Not all was lost, though. Children's Services removed her from Mother Jen's custody, placed her in the care of a nice family from up near Green Bay.

She could have saved Stanley, sure enough; a well-placed slap would have yanked the man from his slumber. Jamie knew it in her heart.

But that's water under the bridge.

She'd never shed a tear for that man.

Ever!

The loss wasn't hers to lament.

# And a Little Child Shall Lead Them

When Daddy said, "Don't look at her, Mattie," he meant the dirty lady in the park near the ice cream stand. But I didn't see any harm in a quick peek in her direction. It's not like she might be a witch, ready to turn me into a flying monkey just because I saw her with my own two eyes.

Problem is, a peek turned into a gawk—a gawk of which *she* became aware!

"Why are you staring at me, little girl?" the grubby old woman asked, coming closer to me and Daddy, right where we were standing, waiting in line for our ice cream cones.

I tried to play like I hadn't even noticed her.

She knew better, though. "You got a cigarette for me?" she asked Daddy.

Daddy doesn't smoke, though. And he said as much.

Her dull gray gaze attached itself to me again. "What about you, Shirley Temple? Can you spare a puff?"

"I don't smoke," I told her, trying my hardest not to stare. "Who's Shirley Temple?"

Daddy interrupted, said, "I'll tell you all about Shirley Temple when we get home, Mattie."

The lady didn't take any of Daddy's hints—like the way he just practically ignored her. She doubled down and went to talking at me like maybe somehow I owed her that cigarette she so badly wanted. "How is it you don't smoke, little Mattie?"

Just hearing my name spoken through her lips put a startle inside of my chest—like when Mrs. Dandell calls on me to answer a question in front of the whole class, knowing full-well I was too busy talking to Allison Spitzley and couldn't possibly know the answer.

"I don't smoke because I'm only eight years old," I heard myself tell her.

She made that *tisk-tisk* sound Mama hates to hear coming from me when I'm having one of my moods.

The lady said, "I smoked my first cigarette when I was just your age. Didn't do *me* any harm."

Her bones rattled in protest against a deep cough that jumped from her mouth.

The man inside the ice cream shop stuck his head through the little window, grabbed at the lady with just his gaze, and said, "Is she bothering you folks?"

Daddy started to register his own complaint, but I jumped in first and told the ice cream man to mind his own business. Well, I didn't say it *exactly* that way—I'm not looking to get the paddle.

"She's not bothering anybody," is what I actually said to the man.

Dirty looks fell on me from Daddy.

I didn't care, though. The lady didn't have anywhere to live—from the looks of it.

Greasy hair that might have been blond—like mine—hung down to her shoulders in a crooked cut. Blue jeans with holes in the knees stayed put only because of a length of rope tied around her waist. The shirt, though, that belonged to a man called Freddie. It even said so on the patch just above her heart. The patch on the other side read *Sunoco.* Gray as her eyes, that shirt—except for big old oil spots tossed here and there.

"Okay, you don't have a cigarette," she said, tugging at those jeans, fighting to keep them from letting her down. "How about a dollar? Can you spare a buck?"

The smell coming off her reminded me of Teddy Kominski's poodle named Turks—back when he got the mange and stunk up the room whenever he came inside the house.

I didn't have a dollar. I only carried the five-dollar bill Daddy gave me for my allowance just this morning. And I intended to spend *that* over to the arcade.

"Who gave you that ring?" I asked, meaning the big sparkly stone on her left hand. I really only meant to make her forget about asking me for money.

Her eyes approached the jewel as if seeing it for the very first time. "This," she said in a tone as soft as my cat Lucy, "came from my husband Bennie."

Daddy put in our order—two cones, both cookie dough ice cream—and waited at the window, certain to keep his eyes on the old lady.

"You have a husband?" I asked, looking around like I might actually see him waiting somewhere in that park.

"Not no more, I don't." Her hand slipped behind her, as if trying to hide. "He got off to somewhere a long time ago. I ain't seen him in a coon's age."

"Is it a real diamond?" I didn't mean to be nosy; it just seems she could sell it and get enough money to last for a while.

"Zirconia. Bennie always was a cheapskate."

"Time to head over to the arcade," Daddy announced, handing me my ice cream cone.

I waited until he went back for napkins before asking the lady about where she lives.

"I sleep in a mansion, little girl," she said, spreading her arms wide. "This park is all mine when the sun goes down."

I don't know about most people, but the idea of somebody having nobody bothers me even worse than stupid old Jimmy Swayzak bothers me at recess—and Jimmy's plenty bad enough, let me tell you.

I asked, "You sleep in the park?"

She dropped a nod.

I dug deeper. "All alone?"

Another nod fell to the ground between us.

Daddy took to talking to Mr. Cromartie, the park policeman, like maybe he no longer felt the need to keep an eye on the lady.

My hand slipped inside my dress pocket; crisp paper teased my fingertips. "How'd you come to be all alone in this world?"

Certainly not the sort of question an eight-year-old girl ought to be asking a grown-up.

The lady, she took no offense in the matter. She said, "I don't really know. It all happened so suddenly."

Daddy's attention discovered me all over again. He hollered, "Come on, Mattie girl; let's go spend your allowance."

It happened so quickly, the way my hand flew from my pocket, money and all, and landed in the lady's hand. "Take this," I said, scrambling toward my father.

"You don't ever want to talk to people like that," Daddy said, aiming us toward the arcade. "We know nothing about her."

Usually, I always trust Daddy, him being a preacher and all. But in this, well—I suspect even preachers can be wrong sometimes!

# MR. WOODLICK

I turned twenty one on October 18, 1977. Charlie Woodlick bought me my first legal taste of alcohol. He taught me how to drink it, as well.

"This is a single malt Scotch, Jimmy," he said, setting the small glass in front of me. "Only take two ice cubes—more than that will water it down."

My eyes absorbed the ambiance of the tiny neighborhood bar on Woodward Avenue in Downtown Detroit.

"You sip it," Charlie explained. "Let it wash across the tongue. Don't ever be a pig about it, Jimmy; gulping a great Scotch is a sin."

I reached for the drink.

Charlie's big meaty hand stopped me. "Let the glass sweat a little first."

Half a dozen fellow patrons occupied seats along the antique oak bar. A television in the corner gave us a look at game six of the World Series: Yankees versus Dodgers. My beloved Detroit Tigers had finished another miserable season; I didn't care who won this fall's classic.

"Used to bring my late wife in here," Charlie remembered. "Every Friday night we'd have a couple of drinks, play a few songs on the juke box, and every so often we'd have us a dance or two."

I wouldn't call Charlie old; I'd guess him to be my grandfather's age. Today, he just looked older, grayer, maybe a little slower.

"When did she die?" I asked, meaning his wife.

"Back in sixty-five—the year before I moved in next to your family."

My gaze settled on that glass aglow with its amber hue. "How long were you married?"

"Twenty years, I guess. I didn't ever really keep track of time back in those days."

"Bet you miss her, huh?"

"Naw." Charlie slipped a Marlboro between his lips, snatched up a book of matches. "She was a bloodsucking bitch." The orange glow of sudden match fire illuminated the dim space—but only for a moment.

Images flickered on the television screen. Fourth inning; Yankees outfielder Reggie Jackson hit the first pitch he saw from Dodgers pitcher Burt Hooton into the stands. A home run for Mr. October.

"Go ahead," Charlie ordered, "pick up your glass."

It came cool to my hand.

"Sip it," Charlie reminded me.

A smoky taste found my tongue; a heat warmed my blood. I'd need time to acquire a fondness for this drink that brought Charlie Woodlick so much joy.

He asked about my girlfriend Gina—was I serious about her?

"*She's* serious," I explained, "but I'm not. I'm too busy trying to figure out how to pay for next semester's tuition. Wayne State isn't cheap."

Charlie knew my situation. He'd helped where he could after my father died.

A second sip from my drink set me in a relaxed mood, chased away the worries from inside my head.

"Scotch is a man's drink," Charlie opined. "I won't mess with anything else."

The fifth inning came around and Reggie Jackson was at it again on the TV. This time he took the first pitch he saw from Elias Sosa deep. A two-run shot. Chants of *Reg-gie! Reg-gie! Reg-gie!* rained down from the Yankee Stadium faithful.

Charlie shifted on his stool, pulled a sip from his glass, and stubbed his spent cigarette into the ashtray. Notions of the worrying sort wandered through his head, left him with a faraway visage.

I didn't mean to pry, what with Charlie being a private person and all; the words just came out. "Is something bothering you, Mr. Woodlick?"

Roy, the old man behind the bar, brought the bottle. "You ready for another, Charlie?" he asked.

Charlie waved him off, waited until Roy had moved on to another customer down the line. "Jimmy," he began, "did I ever tell you about the time I killed a man?"

He hadn't. I'd have certainly remembered a story about a killing. Charlie had a million stories, and I could easily recall most of those he'd shared with me.

"Was it an accident?" I asked.

Charlie's head wagged side to side.

"Bet it happened in the war, huh?

"No, Jimmy. I never served."

I couldn't see my neighbor as any kind of cold-blooded killer. It just didn't fit the person I'd come to know over the last ten years.

"I shot and killed a bank guard during a robbery back in thirty-four," Charlie Woodlick confessed.

A low hum filled my head, blocked out the word selection I desperately needed to peruse.

"How much time did you get?" I asked, finally getting my thoughts around a loose sentence.

"Never got caught." His gaze slipped easily from his near-empty glass and fixed on me. "It was him or me. I didn't think it should be me on that day."

The warmth from the Scotch had me in a good place. I pulled down on another sip, sent a few words in his direction. "Does anybody else know?"

"The FBI—but they're looking for Robert Coppleman, not Charlie Woodlick."

"Did your wife know?"

"She knew."

"Why tell me?"

Charlie's grin brought back the old man whose lawn I'd mowed throughout my high school years. "I want you to turn me in."

I lifted my glass, committed sin-by-gulp, drained it to the dregs. "Why would you want me to turn you in?"

Cancer, he explained. Pancreatic. The worst possible outcome.

Charlie Woodlick would be dead inside of six months.

My hand took on a notion of its own, flagged old Roy and his bottle to my end of the bar.

"Why would you want to die in prison?" I asked once Roy moved on.

"There's a reward, Jimmy. Ten grand, it was, back in thirty-four. It might be more—what with it being forty-three years between then and now. It'll help you and your mother."

I said, "You're just looking to ease your conscience."

"I'm trying to help you out. Look, *somebody* ought to claim that money. Why shouldn't it be you?"

"And you?" I tried to reconcile this man with the one Charlie just introduced me to. Pieces just didn't fit—no matter how hard I tried to force them into place.

"I'll be gone before it gets to trial."

Charlie Hough came at Reggie with a knuckler in the eighth inning. That, too, found the seats. Three home runs in a single World Series game! Not since Babe Ruth…

"I'll have to think it over, Mr. Woodlick," I said, sliding off my stool.

Outside on the street the cool October air dulled my buzz.

I buttoned my coat against the night.

I never again set eyes on Charlie Woodlick.

# A Life Lived (In Under 600 Words)

"My twelfth birthday," said Megan Span, pressing that sealed envelope into David Bellman's hand. "—but only because my mom says I *have* to invite you."

David understood just fine. Girls like Megan were in love with boys like Shaun Cassidy, Andy Gibb, and Leif Garrett. A boy like David Bellman, well, he'd probably end up the booby prize for some fat girl with a lazy eye and a fondness for garlic.

"You have to go," David's mother told him. "It's not polite to turn down an invitation."

Saturday afternoon found ten girls and six boys all squeezed into the Span family basement. Stephanie Kelso suggested games of spin the bottle.

"You *have* to play," Stephanie demanded after David tried to back out. "That's the rules."

"Fine," the boy huffed, giving the Pepsi bottle a quick turn.

Megan rolled her eyes and leaned in for her kiss. "No French, either," she ordered, tucking loose strands of blond hair behind her ears.

David met her above the bottle, pressed his lips to hers—not at all different from the sort of kiss he'd given his mother and grandmother a hundred times. But this one felt softer, tasted of bubblegum-flavored lip gloss.

Megan's blue-eyed gaze fixed onto the boy for just a lingering moment. "Maybe," she said, soft enough to be a whisper.

"Maybe *what?*" David demanded to know this possibility, this potential.

*Do you like me? Circle YES or NO.*

David circled yes on the note Megan handed him on the school bus the following Monday morning.

Four years later, sweet sixteen and Megan made promises. The back seat of David's Camaro provided the setting. Those kisses ran deeper by then—the sort of kisses that swore to be forever.

But David's the one who backed down. "Not like this," he said. "Not in a car."

Megan traded a nod for his rejection.

Senior prom. Young couples danced to The Thompson Twins, Duran Duran, Cutting Crew.

David slipped a whisper into Megan's ear, told of a room waiting for them at the Benchmark Hotel—if she wanted it.

Kisses turned to touching, touching became the giving away of that thing neither could ever take back—no matter what.

"I'm late," Megan said a week after graduation.

"Late for what?" David asked.

A playful punch to his shoulder put the boy right.

"What about college?" he wondered aloud.

"You can still go—if you want."

Megan's parents paid for the small wedding; her father hired David in at the auto dealership.

The ultrasound showed it there on that tiny screen. There were no arms or legs or head; no tears of joy.

There would never be a baby.

Instead of baby names being bandied about, words like *malignant* and *metastasized* filled the small examination room.

Chemo made her hair come out in clumps. Knives scarred her body.

"Move forward," she told David in those last quiet moments. "Don't you die too."

A hole opened in him just wide enough for part of his soul to escape.

He'd never see that hole close up, either. Wounds like this just don't heal.

Stephanie Kelso held his hand at the funeral, kept him from tumbling into the open ground.

"Life will never be the same," David lamented once the service ended.

Stephanie said, "It never is—when somebody dies. That's part of the deal."

David fixed on her blue eyes, found a familiar comfort there. "Think maybe you might wanna go for a cup of coffee?"

# Remaining Ruth

I heard my mother say, "It could be she's just that kind of girl."

I knew she meant me because my father responded, "No daughter of *mine* will be that kind of girl."

I'm an only child, so forget any misunderstandings. Besides, just what kind of girl were they debating me to be?

I slipped through the back door, just inside the kitchen, crouched low near the refrigerator, and listened to their talk in the next room. I'm either a lesbian or a drug addict, depending on their deciphering of my mood on any given day.

Okay. True. I do keep my hair cut short and dyed black. I also prefer jeans and T-shirts to dresses and skirts. But that doesn't make me a lesbian. Of course, there *is* that other thing…

My father said, "Maybe we should send her to one of those Catholic schools."

"We're not Catholic, Fred," my mother reminded him.

"But they know how to deal with these sorts of things, Miriam."

What sorts of things? I wondered, angling for a closer peek into the living room. I didn't need to see, though. My father would be parked in his recliner, newspaper open and held in front of him. My mother, she'd be seated on the sofa, watching the television with the sound turned all the way down.

I'd never get past them. At least not without a hundred questions tossed in my face.

"Maybe we should just leave her be," my mother offered. "I had my own moody moments at that age."

A low *harrumph*, is all my father managed.

As much as I hated the idea of confrontation, I despised even more the notion of hiding out in the kitchen all night.

He's the one who caught me, came right up out of his recliner as soon as I entered the room. "Let's see what's in your pockets, young lady."

I knew the drill. They'd been doing this since the end of the school year, when I'd been stupid enough to leave a joint in my jacket, where my nosy mother happened upon it.

"I'm not carrying," I told my father. "I smoked it before I came in."

"So disrespectful," my mother lamented. "I never sassed *my* parents when *I* was fourteen."

"Gonna let them nuns straighten you out," my father threatened, searching the pockets of my jean jacket.

He found nothing incriminating. I'd learned to never carry anything on me—at least not where they'd bother to look.

"Can I go to my room now?" I asked, not really looking for that argument my parents seemed to enjoy so much.

My father gave up a subtle nod I'd have missed if I hadn't been looking for it.

They took my phone—and my bedroom door.

But I still had the bathroom.

I closed myself inside, pressed the lock. They'd come knocking in a while, demanding to know what all goes on when they can't see.

They'll never see what they don't really want to see, though.

Muffled voices trickled through the floorboards, putting them still in the living room.

My mother's the one who caught me kissing Megan Vennerhull. That's where the whole lesbian thing came from. But we were just practicing. Megan pretended I was David Skillsky and I, well, I too imagined Megan was really David Skillsky—I just told her I'd been dreaming of Michael Kranshaw to keep her from freaking out. Megan has been in love with David since the third grade. But so have I.

Can't tell that to Megan, though.

My fingers worked at the buttons on my jeans; I tugged them off my hips.

My father never used those multi-bladed razors. "One blade is all it takes," he'd tell the television, whenever one of those commercials touting three blades came on.

I agree. One blade is all it takes.

I twisted the razor's handle, retrieved the shiny blade from its open mouth.

It's not a suicide attempt. I've never wanted to die. It's just something I need, something I dream about when moments of stress find in me an easy target.

And I never cut too deep, either; just enough for bleeding.

Just enough for a taste of pain.

They never look at my hips—or my inner thighs. Nobody looks there. Nobody sees or knows.

My mother's voice disrupted my moment of pleasure. "Are you going to be long in there, honey?"

"Be out in a minute," I assured her, knowing full-well my father would be beside her in short order, threatening to remove even the bathroom door.

A quick cut just beneath my stomach let go that crimson release.

Better than an orgasm, this.

My father intruded; his meaty fists banged against the door. "I'll break this son of a bitch down, Ruthie, you don't open this door!"

"Can I wash my hands first?" I asked, rinsing the blade before returning it to its proper place of honor.

They weren't quick enough—not *this* time, at least. I still owned *one* secret belonging only to me.

One more day I could still be the Ruth *I* wanted to be.

# Jazz Baby (Alternative)

Two of them come to fetch me just before noon—a chubby man and a schoolmarm of a woman, each gone well beyond Mama's and Papa's years. The fella, well, he couldn't be bothered with the whole deal, like maybe he'd done enough in his own sight just to have been talked into driving out to dumpy old Rayford. He stood sentry beside that shiny new black Model T Ford, his beady eyes searching neighboring cotton fields like he just knew somebody of a lower station lurked unseen, waiting for a chance to swipe that fancy piece of machinery from beneath his very nose.

And the lady, she didn't want to be here any more than her companion. Uncertainty clouded her countenance like one of those plagues Moses dealt out in the Bible; the sort that could easily blot out that Mississippi sun, switching afternoon to evening with only the shake of a stick.

Didn't matter much to me. Can't say I wanted them there, either—even if they could help me with my dream.

Mama caught me spying through the parlor window.

"You gonna just gawk at 'em all the day, Emily Ann, or might you meet 'em at the door?"

Papa's loose chuckle softened the moment.

"Ain't a reason to be scared, Baby," he said, peeking over his morning paper. "Invite the nice folks inside; offer some refreshments."

Panic peeled away a layer of my confidence.

"I ain't ready for this, Papa," I complained, holding fast my position beside that window. "Besides, *we* don't know they're nice. They could have an old soup recipe needing a fresh girl for the mix, for all anybody knows."

Papa's shifting weight sent his ancient oak rocker to squawking protests.

"Too late," he snapped. "A deal's a deal!"

'Cept I ain't the one shook on it.

"Who told Pastor Pritchett to set this up, anyway?"

That newspaper fell away; Papa's tight gaze snatched hold on mine.

"I'm the one set it up. Now get to bein' neighborly before you catch a lickin'!"

Eunice Spatch offered me one of those forced smiles meant to hide her disgust with my station in life. Those rheumy gray eyes of hers just picked apart my threadbare sundress.

"Well now," she started, her voice humming through a bulbous whiskey-red nose. "Seems you're quite a bit smaller than I'd imagined." Her sloppy gaze stumbled upon those two bumps pushing against the thin yellow fabric at my chest. "Pastor Pritchett made claim you're thirteen."

Scarlet heat burned my cheeks. A mess of words caught in my throat, kept that invitation inside our home from ever making sound. Uppity rich folks just had a way of stealing my voice.

Mama barged into the moment.

"She's a late bloomer, is all. But that don't mean the child can't sing." She jostled in close to the woman, raised that stupid tray of cookies nobody wanted. "I've made refreshments; come inside for a spell."

Old Eunice Spatch, she didn't disappoint. A wave of her hand dismissed my mother, as if the offering itself proved somehow offensive.

"Can't stay," she said, stepping clear of the proffered treats. "Only came to fit the girl for a proper dress, but the one I brought is too big."

Mama's pride lay in jagged little pieces scattered across our front porch. I hated her for such a show of weakness, for always trying to fit in where folks won't accept her.

I don't reckon her not coming in really mattered much—not to me, anyway. It just meant Eunice Spatch would never set eyes on that battered blue sofa Papa found at the side of the road. She'd walk off without a single laugh-out-loud tale of sagging floorboards or that constant smell of bacon leavings clinging to the walls. And nobody would ever have to know that the Teegarten home lacked indoor plumbing and electricity.

Only colored folks had it worse.

"I'll have to trade the dress for something smaller," said the marmish woman. Her long, thin fingers fit snugly beneath my chin, raised my downcast gaze to meet hers. "Awful pretty girl, you are. I've never seen eyes so green—like a china doll's."

That subtle smile teasing the corners of my mouth had nothing at all to do with her stupid compliment—if that's what she intended.

"I ain't wore a new dress in such a while," I confessed, drifting back a few summers when the very garment covering my body still had color to it.

"Yes, well . . ." Eunice Spatch latched onto Mama's arm and pulled her close, like just maybe she still had a chance. "Bathe the child, please. And wash her hair; it's filthy."

*    *    *

That shiny black Ford mocked me from our driveway. They were back already, just waiting to take me away from all I'd ever known. I know we ain't supposed to hate on folks, but these two—well, even Jesus Himself might be hard-pressed to scratch up a kind word.

Papa's the one had the notion to send me over to Jackson. "Use that voice," he said, "—get you someplace ain't Mississippi."

'Cept nobody but church folks enjoy spirituals.

I hugged tight the corner of the house, stayed put behind the lilac bush in hopes they'd think I'd run off and that would be the end of it.

'Cept Mama couldn't be fooled. She flung a handful of words through an open window, promised all sorts of trouble for my backside if I didn't get in that car.

I gained the back steps, met her in the kitchen.

"Ain't a reason you can't do this, Baby," said Mama, pressing a kiss to my forehead. "Now go on and get those people out of my house."

"Come with me," I begged.

"Can't, Baby. You know that."

"Why not?" Seemed I'd asked that question an awful lot lately.

"Papa will come fetch you when it's over."

Suppose it's never over—what then? They might offer me the opening, and that would be it—I'd never see home again.

I let the front door slam in my wake—not out of anger, mind you, but just enough of a bang to let stand my last protest.

Chubby fella helped me into the back seat of Henry Ford's finest. "Won't take long at all to get us there," he promised, sliding behind the wheel.

Enuice Spatch took perch beside him up front, though I can't say if they were husband and wife or only friendly. Every now and again she'd snatch a peek of him, like just maybe they two shared some connected secret might could ruin the both of them should another party trap knowledge of it.

A warm breeze slipped past the open windows, set my hair to wiggling like a loose flapper in a noisy speakeasy.

The man found me in his rearview mirror. "And what are your plans, young lady?"

"Plans?" Lord a-mercy! Did he really need to know?

"Suppose you're the chosen girl. How do you intend to use this experience?—once you've graduated, of course."

I reckon this is what Pastor Pritchett might refer to as a moment of honesty. I blurted, "I'm going to New York to sing jazz."

Their useless opinions landed willy-nilly on either side of me.

"Sodom on the Hudson!" he exclaimed.

"The *devil's* music!" spat Eunice Spatch.

I sifted a pile of words inside my head, tried for my true voice.

"It's nineteen twenty-five," I said. "Things are different now. Girls don't have to get married off and get in a family way just because someone expects us to. We got the vote now. We can be whatever we want." It got good to me. I took hold on his burning gaze in that mirror and jabbed him with my truth. "Won't be long till there's a woman in the White House telling us what's what!"

Scornful laughter twisted my newfound confidence into a knot even Houdini himself couldn't untangle.

"And then what?" bellowed the chubby fella. "A Negro president?" He found third gear and slung us like a stone toward our destination. "You're a dreamer, little girl—a silly dreamer."

Eunice Spatch kept up her cackling as if she'd given ear to vaudeville's best funnyman. I slouched low in my seat, intending to disappear altogether, leaving those two to wonder if maybe I'd been nothing more than a ghost, a vapor of smoke. 'Cept life ain't built that way.

Jackson, Mississippi, came at us quicker than a sucker punch to a blind man's nose, put me to gawking wide-eyed and stupid at crowds of folks scattered here and there along either side of Main Street. Fancy storefronts offered stylish dresses and handsome suits come straight from New York. Flappers gathered at a sidewalk cafe and boldly sucked cigarettes between brightly painted lips. Klaxons sounded warnings, fellas hollered to one another, and somewhere above that cacophony a colored man breathed smoky notes from a battered old saxophone. Didn't need to see it to imagine such a scene.

But then that high steeple breached the pale blue sky and yanked me back to the business at hand.

Eunice Spatch leapt from the car like the fires of hell got on her.

"Hurry up, child!" she demanded, as if she herself had stake in this whole foolish notion. "Can't keep Professor Duncan waiting."

My shoes banged a hasty rhythm against the cement walk. White-haired church ladies milled about the foyer, intent on a thorough lookyloo. I didn't belong in their fancy church; that seemed to be the prevailing opinion.

’Cept I didn’t come for their benefit.

“Can we just get this over with?” I asked.

Eunice Spatch jerked me into a small room just off the foyer and slammed the door shut. “Don’t be an ingrate,” she scolded. “It’s not often a girl from your station is presented with this sort of opportunity.”

A white-haired lady intruded, armed with a pink summer dress just happened to be my size. “Put this on,” she ordered.

In that dress, I could be a whole ’nother girl.

*     *     *

Stanley Duncan pranced about the pulpit like a newly minted deity demanding worship. He gave a nudge to his gold-rimmed spectacles, slid them up the bridge of his pointy nose, and laid down a beady-eyed gawk meant to figure me out on sight alone. His words spilled out in one of those highfalutin’ Yankee tones.

“Well, get on up here, child. We haven’t got all afternoon.”

It’s called a scholarship, he explained, an opportunity to learn proper vocal technique in his school over to Atlanta.

My fingers stroked that delicate pink fabric.

“I already know how to sing,” I told him, suddenly certain of myself.

Whispers and giggles fluttered a-loose in that hot June air.

I didn’t wait for direction or permission; I just faced down those scoffers and fed them “Amazing Grace.” Those mournful words scattered like seeds tossed on thorny ground, almost certain to reach rich soil underneath, the way they always did in the church back home. One by one those white-haired ladies drew out fancy handkerchiefs to dab at stray tears.

Why cry at such a song? Isn’t music supposed to be joyous? I mean, tap your foot if you must. Hum along, even; just please don’t cry.

“Decent,” said Stanley Duncan. “You sound a bit too Negro for a white child—but no need to worry; we can train the heathen from your voice."

*   *   *

I drifted along the sidewalk, toward the corner of Main Street. My fingers smoothed away a wrinkle in that ratty old sundress gone awful comfortable against my bones.

That scholarship belonged to me—if I wanted it.

Should have seen the look on his face when I said no.

"So how'd it go, Baby?" Papa asked, once I climbed into his truck. "Just fine," I told him, watching that colored man blowing his saxophone on the sidewalk.

"Did you get it?"

I tucked up beneath his arm, breathed in his familiar scent.

"Nope," I said softly. "They didn't want me, Papa. They wanted someone willing to be somebody else."

# The Fresh Ink Group

Publishing
Memberships
Share & Read Free Stories, Essays, Articles
Free-Story Newsletter
Writing Contests

Books
E-books
Amazon Bookstore

Authors
Editors
Artists
Professionals
Publishing Services
Publisher Resources

Members' Websites
Members' Blogs
Social Media

www.FreshInkGroup.com

**Email:** info@FreshInkGroup.com

**Twitter: @FreshInkGroup**

**Google+: Fresh Ink Group**

**Facebook.com/FreshInkGroup**

**LinkedIn: Fresh Ink Group**

**About.me/FreshInkGroup**

**JAZZ BABY**

By Beem Weeks

While all Mississippi bakes in the scorching summer of 1925, a sudden orphanhood casts its icy shadow across Emily Ann Teegarten, a pretty young teen.

Taken in by an aunt bent on ridding herself of this unexpected burden, "Baby" Teegarten plots her escape using the only means at her disposal: a voice that makes church ladies cry and angels take notice. "I'm gonna sing jazz up to New York City," she brags to anybody who'll listen. 'Cept that Big Apple—well, it's an awful long way from that dry patch of earth she used to call home.

So when the smoky stages of New Orleans speakeasies give a whistle, offering all kinda shortcuts, Emily soon learns it's the whorehouses and drug joints promising to tickle more than just a young girl's fancy that can dim a spotlight . . . and knowing the wrong people can snuff it out.

*Jazz Baby* just wants to sing—not fight to stay alive.


www.FreshInkGroup.com
ISBN: 978-1-936442-10-2

# Fresh Ink Group Short Story Showcase #1
## Prize-winning Make-you-think Fiction

Edited by Stephen Geez

Fresh Ink Group showcases 42 compelling prize-winners from its literary and genre short-story contests. Eclectic, daring, subtle, provocative, diverse—this wide-ranging collection by authors from across the USA and around the world transcends the limits of single-theme anthologies to explore the best of many styles and bold new ideas.

Travel through time and space. Experience the Dust Bowl, a dying soldier's love, one distraught boy's mirror, the southern-farm snake, suicidal love lost, politicians run amok, a serial killer's lair, seductive sorcerous charms, a malevolent-house warning, inevitable moon-base death, the vengeful walking corpse, or a Holocaust child's hope, the lament of a life never lived . . .

Discerning story-lovers are invited to listen for the voices of these newly favorite authors in *Fresh Ink Group Short Story Showcase #1*. Keep turning the pages to discover what unexpected delights beckon next.

www.FreshInkGroup.com
ISBN: 978-1-936442-17-1

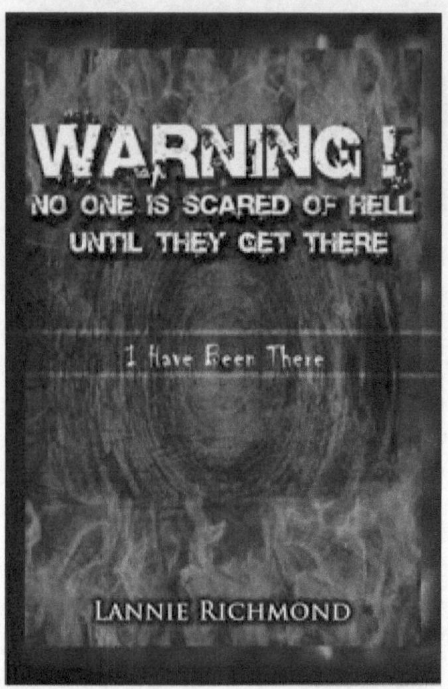


# Warning! No One Is Scared of Hell Until They Get There

## I Have Been There

By Lannie Richmond

I hope you're not like so many people who go through life wanting more and more. People get caught up in living life, never giving a thought to eternity. Everyone will eventually die and find out the truth about what happens after death. God created the soul, which is who we are. Our life is inside our body. The body is only our carrying case for us on this earth. Our soul never dies. Read this book before it's too late for you.

WARNING! NO ONE IS SCARED OF HELL UNTIL THEY GET THERE.

It's a real place and you need to know the truth before you die.

www.FreshInkGroup.com
ISBN: 978-1-936442-19-5

# BEEN THERE, NOTED THAT:

## Essays In Tribute To Life

**Observations, Inspiration, Remembrance,
& Noteworthies To Share**

By Stephen Geez

The simple lives of everyday people in a mundane world prove extraordinary in this collection of 54 personal-experience essays by novelist Stephen Geez. The eclectic mix of memoir, commentary, humor, and appreciation covers a wide range of topics, each beautifully illustrated by artists and photographers from the Fresh Ink Group. Geez catches what many of us miss, then considers how we might all share the most poignant of lessons. *Been There, Noted That* aims to reveal who we are, examine where we've been, and discover what we dare strive to become.

www.FreshInkGroup.com
ISBN: 978-1-936442-05-8

# THE GATES OF VALHALLA

## By Jasper Grawl

From the very beginning of the Universe, to primitive man's invention of Time, through the distant future when countless souls populate vast swaths of empty space, *Valhalla* shows us what really becomes of mankind when we let the politicians run the show.

In an age where farce is the Universe's only unifying principle,  where the only requirement for faster-than-light travel is proper footwear, where a cheap catchphrase and an orange brochure constitute what passes for religion,  Stan has the audacity to resurrect his failing church business by turning the place into a bar and giving his customers what they really want.  Stan's is the only church with the recipe for Salvation.  They sell it on tap.

Meanwhile, crotchety curmudgeon Gumballs finds himself trying to navigate the mind-numbing bureaucracy of the afterlife, his sin-surance policy wholly inadequate, the specter of eternal Hell looming every bit as wretched as an afternoon on C-SPAN.

*The Gates of Valhalla* offers a hilarious yet biting satire on the foibles and fallibilities of everyday people, what they believe, and how they somehow manage to govern their daily lives.  It dares to tackle such trivialities as life and death, heaven and hell, sin and redemption, Earth's corned beef claim to galactic fame, and the very survival of mankind.  Jasper Grawl's side-splitting novel leads you straight to the gates and dares you to step through.

www.FreshInkGroup.com

ISBN: 978-1-936442-18-8

# PAPALA SKIES

By Stephen Geez

Chicago native Rochelle DuFortier likes to imagine the future, her world a series of picture postcards so vivid they sometimes seem real. When a foolish mistake at thirteen causes her mother's death, she's sent to a secluded Hawaiian valley, an outsider "haole-girl" among pidgin-speaking boys who hurl flaming papala spears under the full moon to summon her mother's spirit. After boarding school and a prestigious university back east, the ambitious young woman is torn between chasing new career opportunities, discovering her mother's heritage in a remote French village, and meeting obligations pulling her back to Hawaii.

On this island steeped in ancient mythology and modern superstition, Rochelle tests the possibility of sharing pieces of her life with those whose beliefs she barely understands and never intends to embrace. She dives the depths of a pristine coral lagoon, conceals bodies in a subterranean lava tube, and challenges the eruptions of a living volcano, even as she deciphers the truth about her mother's death and struggles to satisfy new debts born of old betrayals.

*Papala Skies* is the story of a young woman who makes all the right choices, only to find herself living an unexpected life. It is about the need to belong, and seeking one's own version of truth amid such differing cultures' responses to wrenching loss and abiding grief. It is about yearning for a sense of place, yet having to confront new ways to honor the love of family and friends.

Will Rochelle lose what matters most, or might she learn what the smart octopus already knows?

www.FreshInkGroup.com

ISBN: 978-1-936442-07-2